The Twins of Table Mountain and Other Stories

Bret Harte

Contents

CHAPTER I. A CLOUD ON THE MOUNTAIN...7
CHAPTER II. THE CLOUDS GATHER. 14
CHAPTER III. STORM...29
CHAPTER IV. THE CLOUDS PASS...44
PART II. 73
PART III. 80
PART IV. 85
VIEWS FROM A GERMAN SPION 102

THE TWINS OF TABLE MOUNTAIN AND OTHER STORIES

BY

Bret Harte

CHAPTER I.
A CLOUD ON THE MOUNTAIN.

They lived on the verge of a vast stony level, upheaved so far above the surrounding country that its vague outlines, viewed from the nearest valley, seemed a mere cloud-streak resting upon the lesser hills. The rush and roar of the turbulent river that washed its eastern base were lost at that height; the winds that strove with the giant pines that half way climbed its flanks spent their fury below the summit; for, at variance with most meteorological speculation, an eternal calm seemed to invest this serene altitude. The few Alpine flowers seldom thrilled their petals to a passing breeze; rain and snow fell alike perpendicularly, heavily, and monotonously over the granite bowlders scattered along its brown expanse. Although by actual measurement an inconsiderable elevation of the Sierran range, and a mere shoulder of the nearest white-faced peak that glimmered in the west, it seemed to lie so near the quiet, passionless stars, that at night it caught something of their calm remoteness.

The articulate utterance of such a locality should have been a whisper; a laugh or exclamation was discordant; and the ordinary tones of the human voice on the night of the 15th of May, 1868, had a grotesque incongruity.

In the thick darkness that clothed the mountain that night, the human figure would have been lost, or confounded with the outlines of outlying bowlders, which at such times took upon themselves the vague semblance of men and animals. Hence the voices in the following colloquy seemed the more grotesque and incongruous from being the apparent expression of an upright monolith, ten feet high, on the right, and another mass of granite, that, reclining, peeped over the verge.

"Hello!"

"Hello yourself!"

"You're late."

"I lost the trail, and climbed up the slide."

Here followed a stumble, the clatter of stones down the mountain-side, and an oath so very human and undignified that it at once relieved the bowlders of any complicity of expression. The voices, too, were close together now, and unexpectedly in quite another locality.

"Anything up?"

"Looey Napoleon's declared war agin Germany."

"Sho-o-o!"

Notwithstanding this exclamation, the interest of the latter speaker was evidently only polite and perfunctory. What, indeed, were the political convulsions of the Old World to the dwellers on this serene, isolated eminence of the New?

"I reckon it's so," continued the first voice. "French Pete and that thar feller that keeps the Dutch grocery hev hed a row over it; emptied their six-shooters into each other. The Dutchman's got two balls in his leg, and the Frenchman's got an onnessary buttonhole in his shirt-buzzum, and hez caved in."

This concise, local corroboration of the conflict of remote nations, however confirmatory, did not appear to excite any further interest. Even the last speaker, now that he was in this calm, dispassionate atmosphere, seemed to lose his own concern in his tidings, and to have abandoned every thing of a sensational and lower-worldly character in the pines below. There were a few moments of absolute silence, and then another stumble. But now the voices of both speakers were quite patient and philosophical.

"Hold on, and I'll strike a light," said the second speaker. "I brought a lantern along, but I didn't light up. I kem out afore sundown, and you know how it allers is up yer. I didn't want it, and didn't keer to light up. I forgot you're always a little dazed and strange-like when you first come up."

There was a crackle, a flash, and presently a steady glow, which the surrounding darkness seemed to resent. The faces of the two men thus revealed were singularly alike. The same thin, narrow outline of jaw and temple; the same dark, grave eyes; the same brown growth of curly beard and mustache, which concealed the mouth, and hid what might have been any individual idiosyncrasy of thought or expression,--showed them to be brothers, or better known as the "Twins of Table

Mountain." A certain animation in the face of the second speaker,--the first-comer,--a certain light in his eye, might have at first distinguished him; but even this faded out in the steady glow of the lantern, and had no value as a permanent distinction, for, by the time they had reached the western verge of the mountain, the two faces had settled into a homogeneous calmness and melancholy.

The vague horizon of darkness, that a few feet from the lantern still encompassed them, gave no indication of their progress, until their feet actually trod the rude planks and thatch that formed the roof of their habitation; for their cabin half burrowed in the mountain, and half clung, like a swallow's nest, to the side of the deep declivity that terminated the northern limit of the summit. Had it not been for the windlass of a shaft, a coil of rope, and a few heaps of stone and gravel, which were the only indications of human labor in that stony field, there was nothing to interrupt its monotonous dead level. And, when they descended a dozen well-worn steps to the door of their cabin, they left the summit, as before, lonely, silent, motionless, its long level uninterrupted, basking in the cold light of the stars.

The simile of a "nest" as applied to the cabin of the brothers was no mere figure of speech as the light of the lantern first flashed upon it. The narrow ledge before the door was strewn with feathers. A suggestion that it might be the home and haunt of predatory birds was promptly checked by the spectacle of the nailed-up carcasses of a dozen hawks against the walls, and the outspread wings of an extended eagle emblazoning the gable above the door, like an armorial bearing. Within the cabin the walls and chimney-piece were dazzlingly bedecked with the party-colored wings of jays, yellow-birds, woodpeckers, kingfishers, and the poly-tinted wood-duck. Yet in that dry, highly-rarefied atmosphere, there was not the slightest suggestion of odor or decay.

The first speaker hung the lantern upon a hook that dangled from the rafters, and, going to the broad chimney, kicked the half-dead embers into a sudden resentful blaze. He then opened a rude cupboard, and, without looking around, called, "Ruth!"

The second speaker turned his head from the open doorway where he was leaning, as if listening to something in the darkness, and answered abstractedly,--

"Rand!"

"I don't believe you have touched grub to-day!"

Ruth grunted out some indifferent reply.

"Thar hezen't been a slice cut off that bacon since I left," continued Rand, bringing a side of bacon and some biscuits from the cupboard, and applying himself to the discussion of them at the table. "You're gettin' off yer feet, Ruth. What's up?"

Ruth replied by taking an uninvited seat beside him, and resting his chin on the palms of his hands. He did not eat, but simply transferred his inattention from the door to the table.

"You're workin' too many hours in the shaft," continued Rand. "You're always up to some such d--n fool business when I'm not yer."

"I dipped a little west to day," Ruth went on, without heeding the brotherly remonstrance, "and struck quartz and pyrites."

"Thet's you!--allers dippin' west or east for quartz and the color, instead of keeping on plumb down to the 'cement'!"*

     * The local name for gold-bearing alluvial drift,--the bed of a   prehistoric river.

"We've been three years digging for cement," said Ruth, more in abstraction than in reproach,--"three years!"

"And we may be three years more,--may be only three days. Why, you couldn't be more impatient if--if--if you lived in a valley."

Delivering this tremendous comparison as an unanswerable climax, Rand applied himself once more to his repast. Ruth, after a moment's pause, without speaking or looking up, disengaged his hand from under his chin, and slid it along, palm uppermost, on the table beside his brother. Thereupon Rand slowly reached forward his left hand, the right being engaged in conveying victual to his mouth, and laid it on his brother's palm. The act was evidently an habitual, half mechanical one; for in a few moments the hands were as gently disengaged, without comment or expression. At last Rand leaned back in his chair, laid down his knife and fork, and, complacently loosening the belt that held his revolver, threw it and the weapon on his bed. Taking out his pipe, and chipping some tobacco on the table, he said carelessly, "I came a piece through the woods with Mornie just now."

The face that Ruth turned upon his brother was very distinct in its expression at that moment, and quite belied the popular theory that the twins could not be told apart. "Thet gal," continued Rand, without looking up, "is either flighty, or--or suthin'," he added in vague disgust, pushing the table from him as if it were the lady in question. "Don't tell me!"

Ruth's eyes quickly sought his brother's, and were as quickly averted, as he asked hurriedly, "How?"

"What gets me," continued Rand in a petulant non sequitur, "is that YOU, my own twin-brother, never lets on about her comin' yer, permiskus like, when I ain't yer, and you and her gallivantin' and promanadin', and swoppin' sentiments and mottoes."

Ruth tried to contradict his blushing face with a laugh of worldly indifference.

"She came up yer on a sort of pasear."

"Oh, yes!--a short cut to the creek," interpolated Rand satirically.

"Last Tuesday or Wednesday," continued Ruth, with affected forgetfulness.

"Oh, in course, Tuesday, or Wednesday, or Thursday! You've so many folks climbing up this yer mountain to call on ye," continued the ironical Rand, "that you disremember; only you remembered enough not to tell me. SHE did. She took me for you, or pretended to."

The color dropped from Ruth's cheek.

"Took you for me?" he asked, with an awkward laugh.

"Yes," sneered Rand; "chirped and chattered away about OUR picnic, OUR nose-gays, and lord knows what! Said she'd keep them blue-jay's wings, and wear 'em in her hat. Spouted poetry, too,--the same sort o' rot you get off now and then."

Ruth laughed again, but rather ostentatiously and nervously.

"Ruth, look yer!"

Ruth faced his brother.

"What's your little game? Do you mean to say you don't know what thet gal is? Do you mean to say you don't know thet she's the laughing-stock of the Ferry; thet her father's a d----d old fool, and her mother's a drunkard and worse; thet she's got any right to be hanging round yer? You can't mean to marry her, even if you kalkilate to turn me out to do it, for she wouldn't live alone with ye up here. 'Tain't her kind. And if I thought you was thinking of--"

"What?" said Ruth, turning upon his brother quickly.

"Oh, thet's right! holler; swear and yell, and break things, do! Tear round!" continued Rand, kicking his boots off in a corner, "just because I ask you a civil question. That's brotherly," he added, jerking his chair away against the side of the cabin, "ain't it?"

"She's not to blame because her mother drinks, and her father's a shyster," said Ruth earnestly and strongly. "The men who make her the laughing-stock of the Ferry tried to make her something worse, and failed, and take this sneak's revenge on her. 'Laughing-stock!' Yes, they knew she could turn the tables on them."

"Of course; go on! She's better than me. I know I'm a fratricide, that's what I am," said Rand, throwing himself on the upper of the two berths that formed the bedstead of the cabin.

"I've seen her three times," continued Ruth.

"And you've known me twenty years," interrupted his brother.

Ruth turned on his heel, and walked towards the door.

"That's right; go on! Why don't you get the chalk?"

Ruth made no reply. Rand descended from the bed, and, taking a piece of chalk from the shelf, drew a line on the floor, dividing the cabin in two equal parts.

"You can have the east half," he said, as he climbed slowly back into bed.

This mysterious rite was the usual termination of a quarrel between the twins. Each man kept his half of the cabin until the feud was forgotten. It was the mark of silence and separation, over which no words of recrimination, argument, or even explanation, were delivered, until it was effaced by one or the other. This was considered equivalent to apology or reconciliation, which each were equally bound in honor to accept.

It may be remarked that the floor was much whiter at this line of demarcation, and under the fresh chalk-line appeared the faint evidences of one recently effaced.

Without apparently heeding this potential ceremony, Ruth remained leaning against the doorway, looking upon the night, the bulk of whose profundity and blackness seemed to be gathered below him. The vault above was serene and tranquil, with a few large far-spaced stars; the abyss beneath, untroubled by sight or sound. Stepping out upon the ledge, he leaned far over the shelf that sustained their cabin, and listened. A faint rhythmical roll, rising and falling in long undulations against the invisible horizon, to his accustomed ears told him the wind was blowing among the pines in the valley. Yet, mingling with this familiar sound, his ear, now morbidly acute, seemed to detect a stranger inarticulate murmur, as of confused and excited voices, swelling up from the mysterious depths to the stars above, and again swallowed up in the gulfs of silence below. He was roused from a consideration of this phenomenon by a faint glow towards the east, which at last brightened, until the dark outline of the distant walls of the valley stood out against the sky. Were his other senses participating in the delusion of his ears? for with the brightening light came the faint odor of burning timber.

His face grew anxious as he gazed. At last he rose, and re-entered the cabin. His eyes fell upon the faint chalk-mark, and, taking his soft felt hat from his head, with a few practical sweeps of the brim he brushed away the ominous record of their late estrangement. Going to the bed whereon Rand lay stretched, open-eyed, he would have laid his hand upon his arm lightly; but the brother's fingers sought and clasped his own. "Get up," he said quietly; "there's a strange fire in the Canyon head that I can't make out."

Rand slowly clambered from his shelf, and hand in hand the brothers stood upon the ledge. "It's a right smart chance beyond the Ferry, and a piece beyond the Mill, too," said Rand, shading his eyes with his hand, from force of habit. "It's in the woods where--" He would have added where he met Mornie; but it was a point of honor with the twins, after reconciliation, not to allude to any topic of their recent disagreement.

Ruth dropped his brother's hand. "It doesn't smell like the woods," he said slowly.

"Smell!" repeated Rand incredulously. "Why, it's twenty miles in a bee-line yonder. Smell, indeed!"

Ruth was silent, but presently fell to listening again with his former abstraction. "You don't hear anything, do you?" he asked after a pause.

"It's blowin' in the pines on the river," said Rand shortly.

"You don't hear anything else?"

"No."

"Nothing like--like--like--"

Rand, who had been listening with an intensity that distorted the left side of his face, interrupted him impatiently.

"Like what?"

"Like a woman sobbin'?"

"Ruth," said Rand, suddenly looking up in his brother's face, "what's gone of you?"

Ruth laughed. "The fire's out," he said, abruptly re-entering the cabin. "I'm goin' to turn in."

Rand, following his brother half reproachfully, saw him divest himself of his clothing, and roll himself in the blankets of his bed.

"Good-night, Randy!"

Rand hesitated. He would have liked to ask his brother another question; but there was clearly nothing to be done but follow his example.

"Good-night, Ruthy!" he said, and put out the light. As he did so, the glow in the eastern horizon faded, too, and darkness seemed to well up from the depths below, and, flowing in the open door, wrapped them in deeper slumber.

CHAPTER II.
THE CLOUDS GATHER.

Twelve months had elapsed since the quarrel and reconciliation, during which interval no reference was made by either of the brothers to the cause which had provoked it. Rand was at work in the shaft, Ruth having that morning undertaken the replenishment of the larder with game from the wooded skirt of the mountain. Rand had taken advantage of his brother's absence to "prospect" in the "drift,"--a proceeding utterly at variance with his previous condemnation of all such speculative essay; but Rand, despite his assumption of a superior practical nature, was not above certain local superstitions. Having that morning put on his gray flannel shirt wrong side out,--an abstraction recognized among the miners as the sure forerunner of divination and treasure-discovery,--he could not forego that opportunity of trying his luck, without hazarding a dangerous example. He was also conscious of feeling "chipper,"--another local expression for buoyancy of spirit, not common to men who work fifty feet below the surface, without the stimulus of air and sunshine, and not to be overlooked as an important factor in fortunate adventure. Nevertheless, noon came without the discovery of any treasure. He had attacked the walls on either side of the lateral "drift" skilfully, so as to expose their quality without destroying their cohesive integrity, but had found nothing. Once or twice, returning to the shaft for rest and air, its grim silence had seemed to him pervaded with some vague echo of cheerful holiday voices above. This set him to thinking of his brother's equally extravagant fancy of the wailing voices in the air on the night of the fire, and of his attributing it to a lover's abstraction.

"I laid it to his being struck after that gal; and yet," Rand continued to himself, "here's me, who haven't been foolin' round no gal, and dog my skin if I didn't think I heard one singin' up thar!" He put his foot on the lower round of the ladder, paused, and slowly ascended a dozen steps. Here he paused again. All at once the whole shaft was filled with the musical vibrations of a woman's song. Seizing the rope that hung idly from the windlass, he half climbed, half swung himself, to the surface.

The voice was there; but the sudden transition to the dazzling level before him at first blinded his eyes, so that he took in only by degrees the unwonted spectacle of the singer,--a pretty girl, standing on tiptoe on a bowlder not a dozen yards from him, utterly absorbed in tying a gayly-striped neckerchief, evidently taken from her own plump throat, to the halliards of a freshly-cut hickory-pole newly reared as a flag-staff beside her. The hickory-pole, the halliards, the fluttering scarf, the young lady herself, were all glaring innovations on the familiar landscape; but Rand, with his hand still on the rope, silently and demurely enjoyed it.

For the better understanding of the general reader, who does not live on an isolated mountain, it may be observed that the young lady's position on the rock exhibited some study of POSE, and a certain exaggeration of attitude, that betrayed the habit of an audience; also that her voice had an artificial accent that was not wholly unconscious, even in this lofty solitude. Yet the very next moment, when she turned, and caught Rand's eye fixed upon her, she started naturally, colored slightly, uttered that feminine adjuration, "Good Lord! gracious! goodness me!" which is seldom used in reference to its effect upon the hearer, and skipped instantly from the bowlder to the ground. Here, however, she alighted in a POSE, brought the right heel of her neatly-fitting left boot closely into the hollowed side of her right instep, at the same moment deftly caught her flying skirt, whipped it around her ankles, and, slightly raising it behind, permitted the chaste display of an inch or two of frilled white petticoat. The most irreverent critic of the sex will, I think, admit that it has some movements that are automatic.

"Hope I didn't disturb ye," said Rand, pointing to the flag-staff.

The young lady slightly turned her head. "No," she said; "but I didn't know anybody was here, of course. Our PARTY"--she emphasized the word, and accompanied it with a look toward the further extremity of the plateau, to show she was not alone--"our party climbed this ridge, and put up this pole as a sign to show they did it." The ridiculous self-complacency of this record in the face of a man who was evidently a dweller on the mountain apparently struck her for the first time. "We didn't know," she stammered, looking at the shaft from which Rand had emerged, "that--that--" She stopped, and, glancing again towards the distant range where her friends had disappeared, began to edge away.

"They can't be far off," interposed Rand quietly, as if it were the most natural thing in the world for the lady to be there. "Table Mountain ain't as big as all that. Don't you be scared! So you thought nobody lived up here?"

She turned upon him a pair of honest hazel eyes, which not only contradicted the somewhat meretricious smartness of her dress, but was utterly inconsistent with the palpable artificial color of her hair,--an obvious imitation of a certain popular fashion then known in artistic circles as the "British Blonde,"--and began to ostentatiously resume a pair of lemon-colored kid gloves. Having, as it were, thus indicated her standing and respectability, and put an immeasurable distance between herself and her bold interlocutor, she said impressively, "We evidently made a mistake: I will rejoin our party, who will, of course, apologize."

"What's your hurry?" said the imperturbable Rand, disengaging himself from the rope, and walking towards her. "As long as you're up here, you might stop a spell."

"I have no wish to intrude; that is, our party certainly has not," continued the young lady, pulling the tight gloves, and smoothing the plump, almost bursting fingers, with an affectation of fashionable ease.

"Oh! I haven't any thing to do just now," said Rand, "and it's about grub time,

I reckon. Yes, I live here, Ruth and me,--right here."

The young woman glanced at the shaft.

"No, not down there," said Rand, following her eye, with a laugh. "Come here, and I'll show you."

A strong desire to keep up an appearance of genteel reserve, and an equally strong inclination to enjoy the adventurous company of this good-looking, hearty young fellow, made her hesitate. Perhaps she regretted having undertaken a role of such dignity at the beginning: she could have been so perfectly natural with this perfectly natural man, whereas any relaxation now might increase his familiarity. And yet she was not without a vague suspicion that her dignity and her gloves were alike thrown away on him,--a fact made the more evident when Rand stepped to her side, and, without any apparent consciousness of disrespect or gallantry, laid his large hand, half persuasively, half fraternally, upon her shoulder, and said, "Oh, come along, do!"

The simple act either exceeded the limits of her forbearance, or decided the course of her subsequent behavior. She instantly stepped back a single pace, and drew her left foot slowly and deliberately after her; then she fixed her eyes and uplifted eyebrows upon the daring hand, and, taking it by the ends of her thumb and forefinger, lifted it, and dropped it in mid-air. She then folded her arms. It was the indignant gesture with which "Alice," the Pride of Dumballin Village, received the loathsome advances of the bloated aristocrat, Sir Parkyns Parkyn, and had at Marysville, a few nights before, brought down the house.

This effect was, I think, however, lost upon Rand. The slight color that rose to his cheek as he looked down upon his clay-soiled hands was due to the belief that he had really contaminated her outward superfine person. But his color quickly passed: his frank, boyish smile returned, as he said, "It'll rub off. Lord, don't mind that! Thar, now--come on!"

The young woman bit her lip. Then nature triumphed; and she laughed, although a little scornfully. And then Providence assisted her with the sudden presentation of two figures, a man and woman, slowly climbing up over the mountain verge, not far from them. With a cry of "There's Sol, now!" she forgot her dignity and her confusion, and ran towards them.

Rand stood looking after her neat figure, less concerned in the advent of the strangers than in her sudden caprice. He was not so young and inexperienced but that he noted certain ambiguities in her dress and manner: he was by no means impressed by her dignity. But he could not help watching her as she appeared to be volubly recounting her late interview to her companions; and, still unconscious of any impropriety or obtrusiveness, he lounged down lazily towards her. Her humor had evidently changed; for she turned an honest, pleased face upon him, as she girlishly attempted to drag the strangers forward.

The man was plump and short; unlike the natives of the locality, he was closely cropped and shaven, as if to keep down the strong blue-blackness of his beard and hair, which nevertheless asserted itself over his round cheeks and upper lip like a tattooing of Indian ink. The woman at his side was reserved and indistinctive, with that appearance of being an unenthusiastic family servant peculiar to some men's wives. When Rand was within a few feet of him, he started, struck a theatrical attitude, and, shading his eyes with his hand, cried, "What, do me eyes deceive me!" burst into a hearty laugh, darted forward, seized Rand's hand, and shook it briskly.

"Pinkney, Pinkney, my boy! how are you? And this is your little 'prop'? your quarter-section, your country-seat, that we've been trespassing on, eh? A nice little spot, cool, sequestered, remote,--a trifle unimproved; carriage-road as yet unfinished. Ha, ha! But to think of our making a discovery of this inaccessible mountain, climbing it, sir, for two mortal hours, christening it 'Sol's Peak,' getting up a flagpole, unfurling our standard to the breeze, sir, and then, by Gad, winding up by finding Pinkney, the festive Pinkney, living on it at home!"

Completely surprised, but still perfectly good-humored, Rand shook the stranger's right hand warmly, and received on his broad shoulders a welcoming thwack from the left, without question. "She don't mind her friends making free with ME evidently," said Rand to himself, as he tried to suggest that fact to the young lady in a meaning glance.

The stranger noted his glance, and suddenly passed his hand thoughtfully over his shaven cheeks. "No," he said--"yes, surely, I forget--yes, I see; of course you don't! Rosy," turning to his wife, "of course Pinkney doesn't know Phemie, eh?"

"No, nor ME either, Sol," said that lady warningly.

"Certainly!" continued Sol. "It's his misfortune. You weren't with me at Gold Hill.--Allow me," he said, turning to Rand, "to present Mrs. Sol Saunders, wife of the undersigned, and Miss Euphemia Neville, otherwise known as the 'Marysville Pet,' the best variety actress known on the provincial boards. Played Ophelia at Marysville, Friday; domestic drama at Gold Hill, Saturday; Sunday night, four songs in character, different dress each time, and a clog-dance. The best clog-dance on the Pacific Slope," he added in a stage aside. "The minstrels are crazy to get her in 'Frisco. But money can't buy her--prefers the legitimate drama to this sort of thing." Here he took a few steps of a jig, to which the "Marysville Pet" beat time with her feet, and concluded with a laugh and a wink--the combined expression of an artist's admiration for her ability, and a man of the world's scepticism of feminine ambition.

Miss Euphemia responded to the formal introduction by extending her hand frankly with a re-assuring smile to Rand, and an utter obliviousness of her former hauteur. Rand shook it warmly, and then dropped carelessly on a rock beside them.

"And you never told me you lived up here in the attic, you rascal!" continued Sol with a laugh.

"No," replied Rand simply. "How could I? I never saw you before, that I remember."

Miss Euphemia stared at Sol. Mrs. Sol looked up in her lord's face, and folded her arms in a resigned expression. Sol rose to his feet again, and shaded his eyes with his hand, but this time quite seriously, and gazed at Rand's smiling face.

"Good Lord! Do you mean to say your name isn't Pinkney?" he asked, with a half embarrassed laugh.

"It IS Pinkney," said Rand; "but I never met you before."

"Didn't you come to see a young lady that joined my troupe at Gold Hill last month, and say you'd meet me at Keeler's Ferry in a day or two?"

"No-o-o," said Rand, with a good-humored laugh. "I haven't left this mountain for two months."

He might have added more; but his attention was directed to Miss Euphemia, who during this short dialogue, having stuffed alternately her handkerchief, the corner of her mantle, and her gloves, into her mouth, restrained herself no longer, but gave way to an uncontrollable fit of laughter. "O Sol!" she gasped explanatorily, as she threw herself alternately against him, Mrs. Sol, and a bowlder, "you'll kill me yet! O Lord! first we take possession of this man's property, then we claim HIM." The contemplation of this humorous climax affected her so that she was fain at last to walk away, and confide the rest of her speech to space.

Sol joined in the laugh until his wife plucked his sleeve, and whispered something in his ear. In an instant his face became at once mysterious and demure. "I owe you an apology," he said, turning to Rand, but in a voice ostentatiously pitched high enough for Miss Euphemia to overhear: "I see I have made a mistake. A resemblance--only a mere resemblance, as I look at you now--led me astray. Of course you don't know any young lady in the profession?"

"Of course he doesn't, Sol," said Miss Euphemia. "I could have told you that. He didn't even know ME!"

The voice and mock-heroic attitude of the speaker was enough to relieve the general embarrassment with a laugh. Rand, now pleasantly conscious of only Miss Euphemia's presence, again offered the hospitality of his cabin, with the polite recognition of her friends in the sentence, "and you might as well come along too."

"But won't we incommode the lady of the house?" said Mrs. Sol politely.

"What lady of the house"? said Rand almost angrily.

"Why, Ruth, you know!"

It was Rand's turn to become hilarious. "Ruth," he said, "is short for Rutherford, my brother." His laugh, however, was echoed only by Euphemia.

"Then you have a brother?" said Mrs. Sol benignly.

"Yes," said Rand: "he will be here soon." A sudden thought dropped the color from his cheek. "Look here," he said, turning impulsively upon Sol. "I have a brother, a twin-brother. It couldn't be HIM--"

Sol was conscious of a significant feminine pressure on his right arm. He was equal to the emergency. "I think not," he said dubiously, "unless your brother's hair is much darker than yours. Yes! now I look at you, yours is brown. He has a mole on his right cheek hasn't he?"

The red came quickly back to Rand's boyish face. He laughed. "No, sir: my brother's hair is, if any thing, a shade lighter than mine, and nary mole. Come along!"

And leading the way, Rand disclosed the narrow steps winding down to the shelf on which the cabin hung. "Be careful," said Rand, taking the now unresisting hand of the "Marysville Pet" as they descended: "a step that way, and down you go two thousand feet on the top of a pine-tree."

But the girl's slight cry of alarm was presently changed to one of unaffected pleasure as they stood on the rocky platform. "It isn't a house: it's a NEST, and the loveliest!" said Euphemia breathlessly.

"It's a scene, a perfect scene, sir!" said Sol, enraptured. "I shall take the liberty of bringing my scene-painter to sketch it some day. It would do for 'The Mountaineer's Bride' superbly, or," continued the little man, warming through the blue-black border of his face with professional enthusiasm, "it's enough to make a play itself. 'The Cot on the Crags.' Last scene--moonlight--the struggle on the ledge! The Lady of the Crags throws herself from the beetling heights!--A shriek from the depths--a woman's wail!"

"Dry up!" sharply interrupted Rand, to whom this speech recalled his brother's half-forgotten strangeness. "Look at the prospect."

In the full noon of a cloudless day, beneath them a tumultuous sea of pines surged, heaved, rode in giant crests, stretched and lost itself in the ghostly, snow-peaked horizon. The thronging woods choked every defile, swept every crest, filled every valley with its dark-green tilting spears, and left only Table Mountain sunlit and bare. Here and there were profound olive depths, over which the gray hawk hung lazily, and into which blue jays dipped. A faint, dull yellowish streak marked an occasional watercourse; a deeper reddish ribbon, the mountain road and its over-hanging murky cloud of dust.

"Is it quite safe here?" asked Mrs. Sol, eying the little cabin. "I mean from storms?"

"It never blows up here," replied Rand, "and nothing happens."

"It must be lovely," said Euphemia, clasping her hands.

"It IS that," said Rand proudly. "It's four years since Ruth and I took up this yer claim, and raised this shanty. In that four years we haven't left it alone a night, or cared to. It's only big enough for two, and them two must be brothers. It wouldn't do for mere pardners to live here alone,--they couldn't do it. It wouldn't be exactly the thing for man and wife to shut themselves up here alone. But Ruth and me know each other's ways, and here we'll stay until we've made a pile. We sometimes--one of us--takes a pasear to the Ferry to buy provisions; but we're glad to crawl up to the back of old 'Table' at night."

"You're quite out of the world here, then?" suggested Mrs. Sol.

"That's it, just it! We're out of the world,--out of rows, out of liquor, out of cards, out of bad company, out of temptation. Cussedness and foolishness hez got to follow us up here to find us, and there's too many ready to climb down to them things to tempt 'em to come up to us."

There was a little boyish conceit in his tone, as he stood there, not altogether unbecoming his fresh color and simplicity. Yet, when his eyes met those of Miss Euphemia, he colored, he hardly knew why, and the young lady herself blushed rosily.

When the neat cabin, with its decorated walls, and squirrel and wild-cat skins, was duly admired, the luncheon-basket of the Saunders party was re-enforced by provisions from Rand's larder, and spread upon the ledge; the dimensions of the cabin not admitting four. Under the potent influence of a bottle, Sol became hilarious and professional. The "Pet" was induced to favor the company with a recitation, and, under the plea of teaching Rand, to perform the clog-dance with both gentlemen. Then there was an interval, in which Rand and Euphemia wandered a little way down the mountain-side to gather laurel, leaving Mr. Sol to his siesta on a rock, and Mrs. Sol to take some knitting from the basket, and sit beside him.

When Rand and his companion had disappeared, Mrs. Sol nudged her sleeping partner. "Do you think that WAS the brother?"

Sol yawned. "Sure of it. They're as like as two peas, in looks."

"Why didn't you tell him so, then?"

"Will you tell me, my dear, why you stopped me when I began?"

"Because something was said about Ruth being here; and I supposed Ruth was a woman, and perhaps Pinkney's wife, and knew you'd be putting your foot in it by talking of that other woman. I supposed it was for fear of that he denied knowing you."

"Well, when HE--this Rand--told me he had a twin-brother, he looked so frightened that I knew he knew nothing of his brother's doings with that woman, and I threw him off the scent. He's a good fellow, but awfully green, and I didn't want to worry him with tales. I like him, and I think Phemie does too."

"Nonsense! He's a conceited prig! Did you hear his sermon on the world and its temptations? I wonder if he thought temptation had come up to him in the person of us professionals out on a picnic. I think it was positively rude."

"My dear woman, you're always seeing slights and insults. I tell you he's taken a shine to Phemie; and he's as good as four seats and a bouquet to that child next Wednesday evening, to say nothing of the eclat of getting this St. Simeon--what do you call him?--Stalactites?"

"Stylites," suggested Mrs. Sol.

"Stylites, off from his pillar here. I'll have a paragraph in the paper, that the hermit crabs of Table Mountain--"

"Don't be a fool, Sol!"

"The hermit twins of Table Mountain bespoke the chaste performance."

"One of them being the protector of the well-known Mornie Nixon," responded Mrs. Sol, viciously accenting the name with her knitting-needles.

"Rosy, you're unjust. You're prejudiced by the reports of the town. Mr. Pinkney's interest in her may be a purely artistic one, although mistaken. She'll never make a good variety-actress: she's too heavy. And the boys don't give her a fair show. No woman can make a debut in my version of 'Somnambula,' and have the front row in the pit say to her in the sleepwalking scene, 'You're out rather late, Mornie. Kinder forgot to put on your things, didn't you? Mother sick, I suppose, and you're goin' for more gin? Hurry along, or you'll ketch it when ye get home.' Why, you couldn't do it yourself, Rosy!"

To which Mrs. Sol's illogical climax was, that, "bad as Rutherford might be, this Sunday-school superintendent, Rand, was worse."

Rand and his companion returned late, but in high spirits. There was an unnecessary effusiveness in the way in which Euphemia kissed Mrs. Sol,--the one woman present, who UNDERSTOOD, and was to be propitiated,--which did not tend to increase Mrs. Sol's good humor. She had her basket packed all ready for departure; and even the earnest solicitation of Rand, that they would defer their going until sunset, produced no effect.

"Mr. Rand--Mr. Pinkney, I mean--says the sunsets here are so lovely," pleaded Euphemia.

"There is a rehearsal at seven o'clock, and we have no time to lose," said Mrs. Sol significantly.

"I forgot to say," said the "Marysville Pet" timidly, glancing at Mrs. Sol, "that Mr. Rand says he will bring his brother on Wednesday night, and wants four seats in front, so as not to be crowded."

Sol shook the young man's hand warmly. "You'll not regret it, sir: it's a surprising, a remarkable performance."

"I'd like to go a piece down the mountain with you," said Rand, with evident sincerity, looking at Miss Euphemia; "but Ruth isn't here yet, and we make a rule never to leave the place alone. I'll show you the slide: it's the quickest way to go down. If you meet any one who looks like me, and talks like me, call him 'Ruth,' and tell him I'm waitin' for him yer."

Miss Phemia, the last to go, standing on the verge of the declivity, here remarked, with a dangerous smile, that, if she met any one who bore that resemblance, she might be tempted to keep him with her,--a playfulness that brought the ready color to Rand's cheek. When she added to this the greater audacity of kissing her hand to him, the young hermit actually turned away in sheer embarrassment. When he looked around again, she was gone, and for the first time in his experience the mountain seemed barren and lonely.

The too sympathetic reader who would rashly deduce from this any newly awakened sentiment in the virgin heart of Rand would quite misapprehend that peculiar young man. That singular mixture of boyish inexperience and mature doubt and disbelief, which was partly the result of his temperament, and partly of his cloistered life on the mountain, made him regard his late companions, now that they were gone, and his intimacy with them, with remorseful distrust. The mountain was barren and lonely, because it was no longer HIS. It had become a part of the great world, which four years ago he and his brother had put aside, and in which, as two self-devoted men, they walked alone. More than that, he believed he had acquired some understanding of the temptations that assailed his brother, and the poor little vanities of the "Marysville Pet" were transformed into the blandishments of a Circe. Rand, who would have succumbed to a wicked, superior woman, believed he was a saint in withstanding the foolish weakness of a simple one.

He did not resume his work that day. He paced the mountain, anxiously awaiting his brother's return, and eager to relate his experiences. He would go with him to the dramatic entertainment; from his example and wisdom, Ruth should learn how easily temptation might be overcome. But, first of all, there should be the fullest exchange of confidences and explanations. The old rule should be rescinded for once, the old discussion in regard to Mornie re-opened, and Rand, having convinced his brother of error, would generously extend his forgiveness.

The sun sank redly. Lingering long upon the ledge before their cabin, it at last slipped away almost imperceptibly, leaving Rand still wrapped in revery. Darkness, the smoke of distant fires in the woods, and the faint evening incense of the pines, crept slowly up; but Ruth came not. The moon rose, a silver gleam on the farther ridge; and Rand, becoming uneasy at his brother's prolonged absence, resolved to break another custom, and leave the summit, to seek him on the trail. He buckled on his revolvers, seized his gun, when a cry from the depths arrested him. He leaned over the ledge, and listened. Again the cry arose, and this time more distinctly. He held his breath: the blood settled around his heart in superstitious terror. It was the wailing voice of a woman.

"Ruth, Ruth! for God's sake come and help me!"

The blood flew back hotly to Rand's cheek. It was Mornie's voice. By leaning over the ledge, he could distinguish something moving along the almost precipitous face of the cliff, where an abandoned trail, long since broken off and disrupted by the fall of a portion of the ledge, stopped abruptly a hundred feet below him. Rand knew the trail, a dangerous one always: in its present condition a single mis-step would be fatal. Would she make that mis-step? He shook off a horrible temptation that seemed to be sealing his lips, and paralyzing his limbs, and almost screamed to her, "Drop on your face, hang on to the chaparral, and don't move!"

In another instant, with a coil of rope around his arm, he was dashing down the almost perpendicular "slide." When he had nearly reached the level of the abandoned trail, he fastened one end of the rope to a jutting splinter of granite, and began to "lay out," and work his way laterally along the face of the mountain. Presently he struck the regular trail at the point from which the woman must have diverged.

"It is Rand," she said, without lifting her head.

"It is," replied Rand coldly. "Pass the rope under your arms, and I'll get you back to the trail."

"Where is Ruth?" she demanded again, without moving. She was trembling, but with excitement rather than fear.

"I don't know," returned Rand impatiently. "Come! the ledge is already crumbling beneath our feet."

"Let it crumble!" said the woman passionately.

Rand surveyed her with profound disgust, then passed the rope around her waist, and half lifted, half swung her from her feet. In a few moments she began to mechanically help herself, and permitted him to guide her to a place of safety. That reached, she sank down again.

The rising moon shone full upon her face and figure. Through his growing indignation Rand was still impressed and even startled with the change the few last months had wrought upon her. In place of the silly, fanciful, half-hysterical hoyden whom he had known, a matured woman, strong in passionate self-will, fascinating in a kind of wild, savage beauty, looked up at him as if to read his very soul.

"What are you staring at?" she said finally. "Why don't you help me on?"

"Where do you want to go?" said Rand quietly.

"Where! Up there!"--she pointed savagely to the top of the mountain,--"to HIM! Where else should I go?" she said, with a bitter laugh.

"I've told you he wasn't there," said Rand roughly. "He hasn't returned."

"I'll wait for him--do you hear?--wait for him; stay there till he comes. If you won't help me, I'll go alone."

She made a step forward but faltered, staggered, and was obliged to lean against the mountain for support. Stains of travel were on her dress; lines of fatigue and pain, and traces of burning passionate tears, were on her face; her black hair flowed from beneath her gaudy bonnet; and, shamed out of his brutality, Rand placed his strong arm round her waist, and half carrying, half supporting her, began the ascent. Her head dropped wearily on his shoulder; her arm encircled his neck; her hair, as if caressingly, lay across his breast and hands; her grateful eyes were close to his; her breath was upon his cheek: and yet his only consciousness was of the possibly ludicrous figure he might present to his brother, should he meet him with Mornie Nixon in his arms. Not a word was spoken by either till they reached the summit. Relieved at finding his brother still absent, he turned not unkindly toward the helpless figure on his arm. "I don't see what makes Ruth so late," he said. "He's always here by sundown. Perhaps--"

"Perhaps he knows I'm here," said Mornie, with a bitter laugh.

"I didn't say that," said Rand, "and I don't think it. What I meant was, he might have met a party that was picnicking here to-day,--Sol. Saunders and wife, and Miss Euphemia--"

Mornie flung his arm away from her with a passionate gesture. "THEY here!--picnicking HERE!--those people HERE!"

"Yes," said Rand, unconsciously a little ashamed. "They came here accidentally."

Mornie's quick passion had subsided: she had sunk again wearily and helplessly on a rock beside him. "I suppose," she said, with a weak laugh--"I suppose, they talked of ME. I suppose they told you how, with their lies and fair promises, they tricked me out, and set me before an audience of brutes and laughing hyenas to make merry over. Did they tell you of the insults that I received?--how the sins of my parents were flung at me instead of bouquets? Did they tell you they could have spared me this, but they wanted the few extra dollars taken in at the door? No!"

"They said nothing of the kind," replied Rand surlily.

"Then you must have stopped them. You were horrified enough to know that I had dared to take the only honest way left me to make a living. I know you, Randolph Pinkney! You'd rather see Joaquin Muriatta, the Mexican bandit, standing before you to-night with a revolver, than the helpless, shamed, miserable Mornie Nixon. And you can't help yourself, unless you throw me over the cliff. Perhaps you'd better," she said, with a bitter laugh that faded from her lips as she leaned, pale and breathless, against the bowlder.

"Ruth will tell you--" began Rand.

"D--n Ruth!"

Rand turned away.

"Stop!" she said suddenly, staggering to her feet. "I'm sick--for all I know, dying. God grant that it may be so! But, if you are a man, you will help me to your cabin--to some place where I can lie down NOW, and be at rest. I'm very, very tired."

She paused. She would have fallen again; but Rand, seeing more in her face than her voice interpreted to his sullen ears, took her sullenly in his arms, and carried her to the cabin. Her eyes glanced around the bright party-colored walls, and a faint smile came to her lips as she put aside her bonnet, adorned with a companion pinion of the bright wings that covered it.

"Which is Ruth's bed?" she asked.

Rand pointed to it.

"Lay me there!"

Rand would have hesitated, but, with another look at her face, complied.

She lay quite still a moment. Presently she said, "Give me some brandy or whiskey!"

Rand was silent and confused.

"I forgot," she added half bitterly. "I know you have not that commonest and cheapest of vices."

She lay quite still again. Suddenly she raised herself partly on her elbow, and in a strong, firm voice, said, "Rand!"

"Yes, Mornie."

"If you are wise and practical, as you assume to be, you will do what I ask you without a question. If you do it AT ONCE, you may save yourself and Ruth some trouble, some mortification, and perhaps some remorse and sorrow. Do you hear me?"

"Yes."

"Go to the nearest doctor, and bring him here with you."

"But YOU!"

Her voice was strong, confident, steady, and patient. "You can safely leave me until then."

In another moment Rand was plunging down the "slide." But it was past midnight when he struggled over the last bowlder up the ascent, dragging the half-exhausted medical wisdom of Brown's Ferry on his arm.

"I've been gone long, doctor," said Rand feverishly, "and she looked SO death-like when I left. If we should be too late!"

The doctor stopped suddenly, lifted his head, and pricked his ears like a hound on a peculiar scent. "We ARE too late," he said, with a slight professional laugh.

Indignant and horrified, Rand turned upon him.

"Listen," said the doctor, lifting his hand.

Rand listened, so intently that he heard the familiar moan of the river below; but the great stony field lay silent before him. And then, borne across its bare barren bosom, like its own articulation, came faintly the feeble wail of a new-born babe.

III.

STORM.

The doctor hurried ahead in the darkness. Rand, who had stopped paralyzed at the ominous sound, started forward again mechanically; but as the cry arose again more distinctly, and the full significance of the doctor's words came to him, he faltered, stopped, and, with cheeks burning with shame and helpless indignation, sank upon a stone beside the shaft, and, burying his face in his hands, fairly gave way to a burst of boyish tears. Yet even then the recollection that he had not cried since, years ago, his mother's dying hands had joined his and Ruth's childish fingers together, stung him fiercely, and dried his tears in angry heat upon his cheeks.

How long he sat there, he remembered not; what he thought, he recalled not. But the wildest and most extravagant plans and resolves availed him nothing in the face of this forever desecrated home, and this shameful culmination of his ambitious life on the mountain. Once he thought of flight; but the reflection that he would still abandon his brother to shame, perhaps a self-contented shame, checked him hopelessly. Could he avert the future? He MUST; but how? Yet he could only sit and stare into the darkness in dumb abstraction.

Sitting there, his eyes fell upon a peculiar object in a crevice of the ledge beside the shaft. It was the tin pail containing his dinner, which, according to their custom, it was the duty of the brother who staid above ground to prepare and place for the brother who worked below. Ruth must, consequently, have put it there before he left that morning, and Rand had overlooked it while sharing the repast of the strangers at noon. At the sight of this dumb witness of their mutual cares and labors, Rand sighed, half in brotherly sorrow, half in a selfish sense of injury done him.

He took up the pail mechanically, removed its cover, and--started; for on top of the carefully bestowed provisions lay a little note, addressed to him in Ruth's peculiar scrawl.

He opened it with feverish hands, held it in the light of the peaceful moon, and read as follows:

DEAR, DEAR BROTHER,--When you read this, I shall be far away. I go because I shall not stay to disgrace you, and because the girl that I brought trouble upon has gone away too, to hide her disgrace and mine; and where she goes, Rand, I ought to follow her, and, please God, I will! I am not as wise or as good as you are, but it seems the best I can do; and God bless you, dear old Randy, boy! Times and times again I've wanted to tell you all, and reckoned to do so; but whether you was sitting before me in the cabin, or working beside me in the drift, I couldn't get to look upon your honest face, dear brother, and say what things I'd been keeping from you so long. I'll stay away until I've done what I ought to do, and if you can say, "Come, Ruth," I will come; but, until you can say it, the mountain is yours, Randy, boy, the mine is yours, the cabin is yours, ALL is yours. Rub out the old chalk-marks, Rand, as I rub them out here in my--[A few words here were blurred and indistinct, as if the moon had suddenly become dim-eyed too]. God bless you, brother!

P.S.--You know I mean Mornie all the time. It's she I'm going to seek; but don't you think so bad of her as you do, I am so much worse than she. I wanted to tell you that all along, but I didn't dare. She's run away from the Ferry half crazy; said she was going to Sacramento, and I am going there to find her alive or dead. Forgive me, brother! Don't throw this down right away; hold it in your hand a moment, Randy, boy, and try hard to think it's my hand in yours. And so good-by, and God bless you, old Randy!

From your loving brother,
RUTH.

A deep sense of relief overpowered every other feeling in Rand's breast. It was clear that Ruth had not yet discovered the truth of Mornie's flight: he was on his way to Sacramento, and before he could return, Mornie could be removed. Once despatched in some other direction, with Ruth once more returned and under his brother's guidance, the separation could be made easy and final. There was evidently no marriage as yet; and now, the fear of an immediate meeting over, there should be none. For Rand had already feared this; had recalled the few infelicitous relations, legal and illegal, which were common to the adjoining camp,--the flagrantly miserable life of the husband of a San Francisco anonyma who lived in style at the Ferry, the shameful carousals and more shameful quarrels of the Frenchman and Mexican woman who "kept house" at "the Crossing," the awful spectacle of the three half-bred Indian children who played before the cabin of a fellow miner and townsman. Thank Heaven, the Eagle's Nest on Table Mountain should never be pointed at from the valley as another--

A heavy hand upon his arm brought him trembling to his feet. He turned, and met the half-anxious, half-contemptuous glance of the doctor.

"I'm sorry to disturb you," he said dryly; "but it's about time you or somebody else put in an appearance at that cabin. Luckily for HER, she's one woman in a thousand; has had her wits about her better than some folks I know, and has left me little to do but make her comfortable. But she's gone through too much,--fought her little fight too gallantly,--is altogether too much of a trump to be played off upon now. So rise up out of that, young man, pick up your scattered faculties, and fetch a woman--some sensible creature of her own sex--to look after her; for, without wishing to be personal, I'm d----d if I trust her to the likes of you."

There was no mistaking Dr. Duchesne' s voice and manner; and Rand was affected by it, as most people were throughout the valley of the Stanislaus. But he turned upon him his frank and boyish face, and said simply, "But I don't know any woman, or where to get one."

The doctor looked at him again. "Well, I'll find you some one," he said, softening.

"Thank you!" said Rand.

The doctor was disappearing. With an effort Rand recalled him. "One moment, doctor." He hesitated, and his cheeks were glowing. "You'll please say nothing about this down there"--he pointed to the valley--"for a time. And you'll say to the woman you send--"

Dr. Duchesne, whose resolute lips were sealed upon the secrets of half Tuolumne County, interrupted him scornfully. "I cannot answer for the woman--you must talk to her yourself. As for me, generally I keep my professional visits to myself; but--" he laid his hand on Rand's arm--"if I find out you're putting on any airs to that poor creature, if, on my next visit, her lips or her pulse tell me you haven't been acting on the square to her, I'll drop a hint to drunken old Nixon where his daughter is hidden. I reckon she could stand his brutality better than yours. Goodnight!"

In another moment he was gone. Rand, who had held back his quick tongue, feeling himself in the power of this man, once more alone, sank on a rock, and buried his face in his hands. Recalling himself in a moment, he rose, wiped his hot eyelids, and staggered toward the cabin. It was quite still now. He paused on the topmost step, and listened: there was no sound from the ledge, or the Eagle's Nest that clung to it. Half timidly he descended the winding steps, and paused before the door of the cabin. "Mornie," he said, in a dry, metallic voice, whose only indication of the presence of sickness was in the lowness of its pitch,--"Mornie!" There was no reply. "Mornie," he repeated impatiently, "it's me,--Rand. If you want anything, you're to call me. I am just outside." Still no answer came from the silent cabin. He pushed open the door gently, hesitated, and stepped over the threshold.

A change in the interior of the cabin within the last few hours showed a new presence. The guns, shovels, picks, and blankets had disappeared; the two chairs were drawn against the wall, the table placed by the bedside. The swinging-lantern was shaded towards the bed,--the object of Rand's attention. On that bed, his brother's bed, lay a helpless woman, pale from the long black hair that matted her damp forehead, and clung to her hollow cheeks. Her face was turned to the wall, so that the softened light fell upon her profile, which to Rand at that moment seemed even noble and strong. But the next moment his eye fell upon the shoulder and arm that lay nearest to him, and the little bundle, swathed in flannel, that it clasped to her breast. His brow grew dark as he gazed. The sleeping woman moved. Perhaps it was an instinctive consciousness of his presence; perhaps it was only the current of cold air from the opened door: but she shuddered slightly, and, still unconscious, drew the child as if away from HIM, and nearer to her breast. The shamed blood rushed to Rand's face; and saying half aloud, "I'm not going to take your precious babe away from you," he turned in half-boyish pettishness away. Nevertheless he came back again shortly to the bedside, and gazed upon them both. She certainly did look altogether more ladylike, and less aggressive, lying there so still: sickness, that cheap refining process of some natures, was not unbecoming to her. But this bundle! A boyish curiosity, stronger than even his strong objection to the whole episode, was steadily impelling him to lift the blanket from it. "I suppose she'd waken if I did," said Rand; "but I'd like to know what right the doctor had to wrap it up in my best flannel shirt." This fresh grievance, the fruit of his curiosity, sent him away again to meditate on the ledge. After a few moments he returned again, opened the cupboard at the foot of the bed softly, took thence a piece of chalk, and scrawled in large letters upon the door of the cupboard, "If you want anything, sing out: I'm just outside.--RAND." This done, he took a blanket and bear-skin from the corner, and walked to the door. But here he paused, looked back at the inscription (evidently not satisfied with it), returned, took up the chalk, added a line, but rubbed it out again, repeated this operation a few times until he produced the polite postscript,--"Hope you'll be better soon." Then he retreated to the ledge, spread the bear-skin beside the door, and, rolling himself in a blanket, lit his pipe for his night-long vigil. But Rand, although a martyr, a philosopher, and a moralist, was young. In less than ten minutes the pipe dropped from his lips, and he was asleep.

He awoke with a strange sense of heat and suffocation, and with difficulty shook off his covering. Rubbing his eyes, he discovered that an extra blanket had in some mysterious way been added in the night; and beneath his head was a pillow he had no recollection of placing there when he went to sleep. By degrees the events of the past night forced themselves upon his benumbed faculties, and he sat up. The sun was riding high; the door of the cabin was open. Stretching himself, he staggered to his feet, and looked in through the yawning crack at the hinges. He rubbed his eyes again. Was he still asleep, and followed by a dream of yesterday? For there, even in the very attitude he remembered to have seen her sitting at her luncheon on the previous day, with her knitting on her lap, sat Mrs. Sol Saunders! What did it mean? or had she really been sitting there ever since, and all the events that followed only a dream?

A hand was laid upon his arm; and, turning, he saw the murky black eyes and Indian-inked beard of Sol beside him. That gentleman put his finger on his lips with a theatrical gesture, and then, slowly retreating in the well-known manner of the buried Majesty of Denmark, waved him, like another Hamlet, to a remoter part of the ledge. This reached, he grasped Rand warmly by the hand, shook it heartily, and said, "It's all right, my boy; all right!"

"But--" began Rand. The hot blood flowed to his cheeks: he stammered, and stopped short.

"It's all right, I say! Don't you mind! We'll pull you through."

"But, Mrs. Sol! what does she--"

"Rosey has taken the matter in hand, sir; and when that woman takes a matter in hand, whether it's a baby or a rehearsal, sir, she makes it buzz."

"But how did she know?" stammered Rand.

"How? Well, sir, the scene opened something like this," said Sol professionally. "Curtain rises on me and Mrs. Sol. Domestic interior: practicable chairs, table, books, newspapers. Enter Dr. Duchesne,--eccentric character part, very popular with the boys,--tells off-hand affecting story of strange woman--one 'more unfortunate'--having baby in Eagle's Nest, lonely place on 'peaks of Snowdon,' midnight; eagles screaming, you know, and far down unfathomable depths; only attendant, cold-blooded ruffian, evidently father of child, with sinister designs on child and mother."

"He didn't say THAT!" said Rand, with an agonized smile.

"Order! Sit down in front!" continued Sol easily. "Mrs. Sol--highly interested, a mother herself--demands name of place. 'Table Mountain.' No; it cannot be--it is! Excitement. Mystery! Rosey rises to occasion--comes to front: 'Some one must go; I--I--will go myself!' Myself, coming to center: 'Not alone, dearest; I--I will accompany you!' A shriek at right upper center. Enter the 'Marysville Pet.' 'I have heard all. 'Tis a base calumny. It cannot be HE--Randolph! Never!'--'Dare you accompany us will!' Tableau."

"Is Miss Euphemia--here?" gasped Rand, practical even in his embarrassment.

"Or-r-rder! Scene second. Summit of mountain--moonlight Peaks of Snowdon in distance. Right--lonely cabin. Enter slowly up defile, Sol, Mrs. Sol, the 'Pet.' Advance slowly to cabin. Suppressed shriek from the 'Pet,' who rushes to recumbent figure--Left--discovered lying beside cabin-door. ''Tis he! Hist! he sleeps!' Throws blanket over him, and retires up stage--so." Here Sol achieved a vile imitation of the "Pet's" most enchanting stage-manner. "Mrs. Sol advances--Center--throws open door. Shriek! ''Tis Mornie, the lost found!' The 'Pet' advances: 'And the father is?'--'Not Rand!' The 'Pet' kneeling: 'Just Heaven, I thank thee!' No, it is--'"

"Hush!" said Rand appealingly, looking toward the cabin.

"Hush it is!" said the actor good-naturedly. "But it's all right, Mr. Rand: we'll pull you through."

Later in the morning, Rand learned that Mornie's ill-fated connection with the Star Variety Troupe had been a source of anxiety to Mrs. Sol, and she had reproached herself for the girl's infelicitous debut.

"But, Lord bless you, Mr. Rand!" said Sol, "it was all in the way of business. She came to us--was fresh and new. Her chance, looking at it professionally, was as good as any amateur's; but what with her relations here, and her bein' known, she didn't take. We lost money on her! It's natural she should feel a little ugly. We all do when we get sorter kicked back onto ourselves, and find we can't stand alone. Why, you wouldn't believe it," he continued, with a moist twinkle of his black eyes; "but the night I lost my little Rosey, of diphtheria in Gold Hill, the child was down on the bills for a comic song; and I had to drag Mrs. Sol on, cut up as she was, and filled up with that much of Old Bourbon to keep her nerves stiff, so she could do an old gag with me to gain time, and make up the 'variety.' Why, sir, when I came to the front, I was ugly! And when one of the boys in the front row sang out, 'Don't expose that poor child to the night air, Sol,'--meaning Mrs. Sol,--I acted ugly. No, sir, it's human nature; and it was quite natural that Mornie, when she caught sight o' Mrs. Sol's face last night, should rise up and cuss us both. Lord, if she'd only acted like that! But the old lady got her quiet at last; and, as I said before, it's all right, and we'll pull her through. But don't YOU thank us: it's a little matter betwixt us and Mornie. We've got everything fixed, so that Mrs. Sol can stay right along. We'll pull Mornie through, and get her away from this, and her baby too, as soon as we can. You won't get mad if I tell you something?" said Sol, with a half-apologetic laugh. "Mrs. Sol was rather down on you the other day, hated you on sight, and preferred your brother to you; but when she found he'd run off and left YOU, you,--don't mind my sayin',--a 'mere boy,' to take what oughter be HIS place, why, she just wheeled round agin' him. I suppose he got flustered, and couldn't face the music. Never left a word of explanation? Well, it wasn't exactly square, though I tell the old woman it's human nature. He might have dropped a hint where he was goin'. Well, there, I won't say a word more agin' him. I know how you feel. Hush it is."

It was the firm conviction of the simple-minded Sol that no one knew the various natural indications of human passion better than himself. Perhaps it was one of the fallacies of his profession that the expression of all human passion was limited to certain conventional signs and sounds. Consequently, when Rand colored violently, became confused, stammered, and at last turned hastily away, the good-hearted fellow instantly recognized the unfailing evidence of modesty and innocence embarrassed by recognition. As for Rand, I fear his shame was only momentary. Confirmed in the belief of his ulterior wisdom and virtue, his first embarrassment over, he was not displeased with this halfway tribute, and really believed that the time would come when Mr. Sol should eventually praise his sagacity and reservation, and acknowledge that he was something more than a mere boy. He, nevertheless, shrank from meeting Mornie that morning, and was glad that the presence of Mrs. Sol relieved him from that duty.

The day passed uneventfully. Rand busied himself in his usual avocations, and constructed a temporary shelter for himself and Sol beside the shaft, besides rudely shaping a few necessary articles of furniture for Mrs. Sol.

"It will be a little spell yet afore Mornie's able to be moved," suggested Sol, "and you might as well be comfortable."

Rand sighed at this prospect, yet presently forgot himself in the good humor of his companion, whose admiration for himself he began to patronizingly admit. There was no sense of degradation in accepting the friendship of this man who had traveled so far, seen so much, and yet, as a practical man of the world, Rand felt was so inferior to himself. The absence of Miss Euphemia, who had early left the mountain, was a source of odd, half-definite relief. Indeed, when he closed his eyes to rest that night, it was with a sense that the reality of his situation was not as bad as he had feared. Once only, the figure of his brother--haggard, weary, and footsore, on his hopeless quest, wandering in lonely trails and lonelier settlements--came across his fancy; but with it came the greater fear of his return, and the pathetic figure was banished. "And, besides, he's in Sacramento by this time, and like as not forgotten us all," he muttered; and, twining this poppy and mandragora around his pillow, he fell asleep.

His spirits had quite returned the next morning, and once or twice he found himself singing while at work in the shaft. The fear that Ruth might return to the mountain before he could get rid of Mornie, and the slight anxiety that had grown upon him to know something of his brother's movements, and to be able to govern them as he wished, caused him to hit upon the plan of constructing an ingenious advertisement to be published in the San Francisco journals, wherein the missing Ruth should be advised that news of his quest should be communicated to him by "a friend," through the same medium, after an interval of two weeks. Full of this amiable intention, he returned to the surface to dinner. Here, to his momentary confusion, he met Miss Euphemia, who, in absence of Sol, was assisting Mrs. Sol in the details of the household.

If the honest frankness with which that young lady greeted him was not enough to relieve his embarrassment, he would have forgotten it in the utterly new and changed aspect she presented. Her extravagant walking-costume of the previous day was replaced by some bright calico, a little white apron, and a broad-brimmed straw-hat, which seemed to Rand, in some odd fashion, to restore her original girl- ish simplicity. The change was certainly not unbecoming to her. If her waist was not as tightly pinched, a la mode, there still was an honest, youthful plumpness about it; her step was freer for the absence of her high-heel boots; and even the hand she extended to Rand, if not quite so small as in her tight gloves, and a little brown from exposure, was magnetic in its strong, kindly grasp. There was perhaps a slight suggestion of the practical Mr. Sol in her wholesome presence; and Rand could not help wondering if Mrs. Sol had ever been a Gold Hill "Pet" before her marriage with Mr. Sol. The young girl noticed his curious glance.

"You never saw me in my rehearsal dress before," she said, with a laugh. "But I'm not 'company' to-day, and didn't put on my best harness to knock round in. I suppose I look dreadful."

"I don't think you look bad," said Rand simply.

"Thank you," said Euphemia, with a laugh and a courtesy. "But this isn't getting the dinner."

As part of that operation evidently was the taking-off of her hat, the putting- up of some thick blond locks that had escaped, and the rolling-up of her sleeves over a pair of strong, rounded arms, Rand lingered near her. All trace of the "Pet's" previous professional coquetry was gone,--perhaps it was only replaced by a more natural one; but as she looked up, and caught sight of Rand's interested face, she laughed again, and colored a little. Slight as was the blush, it was sufficient to kindle a sympathetic fire in Rand's own cheeks, which was so utterly unexpected to him that he turned on his heel in confusion. "I reckon she thinks I'm soft and silly, like Ruth," he soliloquized, and, determining not to look at her again, betook himself to a distant and contemplative pipe. In vain did Miss Euphemia address herself to the ostentatious getting of the dinner in full view of him; in vain did she bring the coffee-pot away from the fire, and nearer Rand, with the apparent intention of examining its contents in a better light; in vain, while wiping a plate, did she, absorbed in the distant prospect, walk to the verge of the mountain, and become statuesque and forgetful. The sulky young gentleman took no outward notice of her.

Mrs. Sol's attendance upon Mornie prevented her leaving the cabin, and Rand and Miss Euphemia dined in the open air alone. The ridiculousness of keeping up a formal attitude to his solitary companion caused Rand to relax; but, to his astonishment, the "Pet" seemed to have become correspondingly distant and formal. After a few moments of discomfort, Rand, who had eaten little, arose, and "believed he would go back to work."

"Ah, yes!" said the "Pet," with an indifferent air, "I suppose you must. Well, good-by, Mr. Pinkney."

Rand turned. "YOU are not going?" he asked, in some uneasiness.

"I'VE got some work to do too," returned Miss Euphemia a little curtly.

"But," said the practical Rand, "I thought you allowed that you were fixed to stay until to-morrow?"

But here Miss Euphemia, with rising color and slight acerbity of voice, was not aware that she was "fixed to stay" anywhere, least of all when she was in the way. More than that, she MUST say--although perhaps it made no difference, and she ought not to say it--that she was not in the habit of intruding upon gentlemen who plainly gave her to understand that her company was not desirable. She did not know why she said this--of course it could make no difference to anybody who didn't, of course, care--but she only wanted to say that she only came here because her dear friend, her adopted mother,--and a better woman never breathed,--had come, and had asked her to stay. Of course, Mrs. Sol was an intruder herself--Mr. Sol was an intruder--they were all intruders: she only wondered that Mr. Pinkney had borne with them so long. She knew it was an awful thing to be here, taking care of a poor--poor, helpless woman; but perhaps Mr. Rand's BROTHER might forgive them, if he couldn't. But no matter, she would go--Mr. Sol would go--ALL would go; and then, perhaps, Mr, Rand--

She stopped breathless; she stopped with the corner of her apron against her tearful hazel eyes; she stopped with--what was more remarkable than all--Rand's arm actually around her waist, and his astonished, alarmed face within a few inches of her own.

"Why, Miss Euphemia, Phemie, my dear girl! I never meant anything like THAT," said Rand earnestly. "I really didn't now! Come now!"

"You never once spoke to me when I sat down," said Miss Euphemia, feebly endeavoring to withdraw from Rand's grasp.

"I really didn't! Oh, come now, look here! I didn't! Don't! There's a dear-- THERE!"

This last conclusive exposition was a kiss. Miss Euphemia was not quick enough to release herself from his arms. He anticipated that act a full half-second, and had dropped his own, pale and breathless.

The girl recovered herself first. "There, I declare, I'm forgetting Mrs. Sol's coffee!" she exclaimed hastily, and, snatching up the coffee-pot, disappeared. When she returned, Rand was gone. Miss Euphemia busied herself demurely in clearing up the dishes, with the tail of her eye sweeping the horizon of the summit level around her. But no Rand appeared. Presently she began to laugh quietly to herself. This occurred several times during her occupation, which was somewhat prolonged. The result of this meditative hilarity was summed up in a somewhat grave and thoughtful deduction as she walked slowly back to the cabin: "I do believe I'm the first woman that that boy ever kissed."

Miss Euphemia staid that day and the next, and Rand forgot his embarrassment. By what means I know not, Miss Euphemia managed to restore Rand's confidence in himself and in her, and in a little ramble on the mountain-side got him to relate, albeit somewhat reluctantly, the particulars of his rescue of Mornie from her dangerous position on the broken trail.

"And, if you hadn't got there as soon as you did, she'd have fallen?" asked the "Pet."

"I reckon," returned Rand gloomily: "she was sorter dazed and crazed like."

"And you saved her life?"

"I suppose so, if you put it that way," said Rand sulkily.

"But how did you get her up the mountain again?"

"Oh! I got her up," returned Rand moodily.

"But how? Really, Mr. Rand, you don't know how interesting this is. It's as good as a play," said the "Pet," with a little excited laugh.

"Oh, I carried her up!"

"In your arms?"

"Y-e-e-s."

Miss Euphemia paused, and bit off the stalk of a flower, made a wry face, and threw it away from her in disgust.

Then she dug a few tiny holes in the earth with her parasol, and buried bits of the flower-stalk in them, as if they had been tender memories. "I suppose you knew Mornie very well?" she asked.

"I used to run across her in the woods," responded Rand shortly, "a year ago. I didn't know her so well then as--" He stopped.

"As what? As NOW?" asked the "Pet" abruptly. Rand, who was coloring over his narrow escape from a topic which a delicate kindness of Sol had excluded from their intercourse on the mountain, stammered, "as YOU do, I meant."

The "Pet" tossed her head a little. "Oh! I don't know her at all--except through Sol."

Rand stared hard at this. The "Pet," who was looking at him intently, said, "Show me the place where you saw Mornie clinging that night."

"It's dangerous," suggested Rand.

"You mean I'd be afraid! Try me! I don't believe she was SO dreadfully frightened!"

"Why?" asked Rand, in astonishment.

"Oh--because--"

Rand sat down in vague wonderment.

"Show it to me," continued the "Pet," "or--I'll find it ALONE!"

Thus challenged, he rose, and, after a few moments' climbing, stood with her upon the trail. "You see that thorn-bush where the rock has fallen away. It was just there. It is not safe to go farther. No, really! Miss Euphemia! Please don't! It's almost certain death!"

But the giddy girl had darted past him, and, face to the wall of the cliff, was creeping along the dangerous path. Rand followed mechanically. Once or twice the trail crumbled beneath her feet; but she clung to a projecting root of chaparral, and laughed. She had almost reached her elected goal, when, slipping, the treacherous chaparral she clung to yielded in her grasp, and Rand, with a cry, sprung forward.

But the next instant she quickly transferred her hold to a cleft in the cliff, and was safe. Not so her companion. The soil beneath him, loosened by the impulse of his spring, slipped away: he was falling with it, when she caught him sharply with her disengaged hand, and together they scrambled to a more secure footing.

"I could have reached it alone," said the "Pet," "if you'd left me alone."

"Thank Heaven, we're saved!" said Rand gravely.

"AND WITHOUT A ROPE," said Miss Euphemia significantly.

Rand did not understand her. But, as they slowly returned to the summit, he stammered out the always difficult thanks of a man who has been physically helped by one of the weaker sex. Miss Euphemia was quick to see her error.

"I might have made you lose your footing by catching at you," she said meekly. "But I was so frightened for you, and could not help it."

The superior animal, thoroughly bamboozled, thereupon complimented her on her dexterity.

"Oh, that's nothing!" she said, with a sigh. "I used to do the flying-trapeze business with papa when I was a child, and I've not forgotten it." With this and other confidences of her early life, in which Rand betrayed considerable interest, they beguiled the tedious ascent. "I ought to have made you carry me up," said the lady, with a little laugh, when they reached the summit; "but you haven't known me as long as you have Mornie, have you?" With this mysterious speech she bade Rand "good-night," and hurried off to the cabin.

And so a week passed by,--the week so dreaded by Rand, yet passed so pleasantly, that at times it seemed as if that dread were only a trick of his fancy, or as if the circumstances that surrounded him were different from what he believed them to be. On the seventh day the doctor had staid longer than usual; and Rand, who had been sitting with Euphemia on the ledge by the shaft, watching the sunset, had barely time to withdraw his hand from hers, as Mrs. Sol, a trifle pale and wearied-looking, approached him.

"I don't like to trouble you," she said,--indeed, they had seldom troubled him with the details of Mornie's convalescence, or even her needs and requirements,--"but the doctor is alarmed about Mornie, and she has asked to see you. I think you'd better go in and speak to her. You know," continued Mrs. Sol delicately, "you haven't been in there since the night she was taken sick, and maybe a new face might do her good."

The guilty blood flew to Rand's face as he stammered, "I thought I'd be in the way. I didn't believe she cared much to see me. Is she worse?"

"The doctor is looking very anxious," said Mrs. Sol simply.

The blood returned from Rand's face, and settled around his heart. He turned very pale. He had consoled himself always for his complicity in Ruth's absence, that he was taking good care of Mornie, or--what is considered by most selfish natures an equivalent--permitting or encouraging some one else to "take good care of her;" but here was a contingency utterly unforeseen. It did not occur to him that this "taking good care" of her could result in anything but a perfect solution of her troubles, or that there could be any future to her condition but one of recovery. But what if she should die? A sudden and helpless sense of his responsibility to Ruth, to HER, brought him trembling to his feet.

He hurried to the cabin, where Mrs. Sol left him with a word of caution: "You'll find her changed and quiet,--very quiet. If I was you, I wouldn't say anything to bring back her old self."

The change which Rand saw was so great, the face that was turned to him so quiet, that, with a new fear upon him, he would have preferred the savage eyes and reckless mien of the old Mornie whom he hated. With his habitual impulsiveness he tried to say something that should express that fact not unkindly, but faltered, and awkwardly sank into the chair by her bedside.

"I don't wonder you stare at me now," she said in a far-off voice. "It seems to you strange to see me lying here so quiet. You are thinking how wild I was when I came here that night. I must have been crazy, I think. I dreamed that I said dreadful things to you; but you must forgive me, and not mind it. I was crazy then." She stopped, and folded the blanket between her thin fingers. "I didn't ask you to come here to tell you that, or to remind you of it; but--but when I was crazy, I said so many worse, dreadful things of HIM; and you--YOU will be left behind to tell him of it."

Rand was vaguely murmuring something to the effect that "he knew she didn't mean anything," that "she musn't think of it again," that "he'd forgotten all about it," when she stopped him with a tired gesture.

"Perhaps I was wrong to think, that, after I am gone, you would care to tell him anything. Perhaps I'm wrong to think of it at all, or to care what he will think of me, except for the sake of the child--his child, Rand--that I must leave behind me. He will know that IT never abused him. No, God bless its sweet heart! IT never was wild and wicked and hateful, like its cruel, crazy mother. And he will love it; and you, perhaps, will love it too--just a little, Rand! Look at it!" She tried to raise the helpless bundle beside her in her arms, but failed. "You must lean over," she said faintly to Rand. "It looks like him, doesn't it?"

Rand, with wondering, embarrassed eyes, tried to see some resemblance, in the little blue-red oval, to the sad, wistful face of his brother, which even then was haunting him from some mysterious distance. He kissed the child's forehead, but even then so vaguely and perfunctorily, that the mother sighed, and drew it closer to her breast.

"The doctor says," she continued in a calmer voice, "that I'm not doing as well as I ought to. I don't think," she faltered, with something of her old bitter laugh, "that I'm ever doing as well as I ought to, and perhaps it's not strange now that I don't. And he says that, in case anything happens to me, I ought to look ahead. I have looked ahead. It's a dark look ahead, Rand--a horror of blackness, without kind faces, without the baby, without--without HIM!"

She turned her face away, and laid it on the bundle by her side. It was so quiet in the cabin, that, through the open door beyond, the faint, rhythmical moan of the pines below was distinctly heard.

"I know it's foolish; but that is what 'looking ahead' always meant to me," she said, with a sigh. "But, since the doctor has been gone, I've talked to Mrs. Sol, and find it's for the best. And I look ahead, and see more clearly. I look ahead, and see my disgrace removed far away from HIM and you. I look ahead, and see you and HE living together happily, as you did before I came between you. I look ahead, and see my past life forgotten, my faults forgiven; and I think I see you both loving my baby, and perhaps loving me a little for its sake. Thank you, Rand, thank you!"

For Rand's hand had caught hers beside the pillow, and he was standing over her, whiter than she. Something in the pressure of his hand emboldened her to go on, and even lent a certain strength to her voice.

"When it comes to THAT, Rand, you'll not let these people take the baby away. You'll keep it HERE with you until HE comes. And something tells me that he will come when I am gone. You'll keep it here in the pure air and sunlight of the mountain, and out of those wicked depths below; and when I am gone, and they are gone, and only you and Ruth and baby are here, maybe you'll think that it came to you in a cloud on the mountain,--a cloud that lingered only long enough to drop its burden, and faded, leaving the sunlight and dew behind. What is it, Rand? What are you looking at?"

"I was thinking," said Rand in a strange altered voice, "that I must trouble you to let me take down those duds and furbelows that hang on the wall, so that I can get at some traps of mine behind them." He took some articles from the wall, replaced the dresses of Mrs. Sol, and answered Mornie's look of inquiry.

"I was only getting at my purse and my revolver," he said, showing them. "I've got to get some stores at the Ferry by daylight."

Mornie sighed. "I'm giving you great trouble, Rand, I know; but it won't be for long."

He muttered something, took her hand again, and bade her "good-night." When he reached the door, he looked back. The light was shining full upon her face as she lay there, with her babe on her breast, bravely "looking ahead."

IV.
THE CLOUDS PASS.

It was early morning at the Ferry. The "up coach" had passed, with lights unextinguished, and the "outsides" still asleep. The ferryman had gone up to the Ferry Mansion House, swinging his lantern, and had found the sleepy-looking "all night" bar-keeper on the point of withdrawing for the day on a mattress under the bar. An Indian half-breed, porter of the Mansion House, was washing out the stains of recent nocturnal dissipation from the bar-room and veranda; a few birds were twittering on the cotton-woods beside the river; a bolder few had alighted upon the veranda, and were trying to reconcile the existence of so much lemon-peel and cigar-stumps with their ideas of a beneficent Creator. A faint earthly freshness and perfume rose along the river banks. Deep shadow still lay upon the opposite shore; but in the distance, four miles away, Morning along the level crest of Table Mountain walked with rosy tread.

The sleepy bar-keeper was that morning doomed to disappointment; for scarcely had the coach passed, when steps were heard upon the veranda, and a weary, dusty traveller threw his blanket and knapsack to the porter, and then dropped into a vacant arm-chair, with his eyes fixed on the distant crest of Table Mountain. He remained motionless for some time, until the bar-keeper, who had already concocted the conventional welcome of the Mansion House, appeared with it in a glass, put it upon the table, glanced at the stranger, and then, thoroughly awake, cried out,--

"Ruth Pinkney--or I'm a Chinaman!"

The stranger lifted his eyes wearily. Hollow circles were around their orbits; haggard lines were in his checks. But it was Ruth.

He took the glass, and drained it at a single draught. "Yes," he said absently, "Ruth Pinkney," and fixed his eyes again on the distant rosy crest.

"On your way up home?" suggested the bar-keeper, following the direction of Ruth's eyes.

"Perhaps."

"Been upon a pasear, hain't yer? Been havin' a little tear round Sacramento,-- seein' the sights?"

Ruth smiled bitterly. "Yes."

The bar-keeper lingered, ostentatiously wiping a glass. But Ruth again became abstracted in the mountain, and the barkeeper turned away.

How pure and clear that summit looked to him! how restful and steadfast with serenity and calm! how unlike his own feverish, dusty, travel-worn self! A week had elapsed since he had last looked upon it,--a week of disappointment, of anxious fears, of doubts, of wild imaginings, of utter helplessness. In his hopeless quest of the missing Mornie, he had, in fancy, seen this serene eminence haunting his remorseful, passion-stricken soul. And now, without a clew to guide him to her unknown hiding-place, he was back again, to face the brother whom he had deceived, with only the confession of his own weakness. Hard as it was to lose forever the fierce, reproachful glances of the woman he loved, it was still harder, to a man of Ruth's temperament, to look again upon the face of the brother he feared. A hand laid upon his shoulder startled him. It was the bar-keeper.

"If it's a fair question, Ruth Pinkney, I'd like to ask ye how long ye kalkilate to hang around the Ferry to-day."

"Why?" demanded Ruth haughtily.

"Because, whatever you've been and done, I want ye to have a square show. Ole Nixon has been cavoortin' round yer the last two days, swearin' to kill you on sight for runnin' off with his darter. Sabe? Now, let me ax ye two questions. FIRST, Are you heeled?"

Ruth responded to this dialectical inquiry affirmatively by putting his hand on his revolver.

"Good! Now, SECOND, Have you got the gal along here with you?"

"No," responded Ruth in a hollow voice.

"That's better yet," said the man, without heeding the tone of the reply. "A woman--and especially THE woman in a row of this kind--handicaps a man awful." He paused, and took up the empty glass. "Look yer, Ruth Pinkney, I'm a square man, and I'll be square with you. So I'll just tell you you've got the demdest odds agin' ye. Pr'aps ye know it, and don't keer. Well, the boys around yer are all sidin' with the old man Nixon. It's the first time the old rip ever had a hand in his favor: so the boys will see fair play for Nixon, and agin' YOU. But I reckon you don't mind him!"

"So little, I shall never pull trigger on him," said Ruth gravely.

The bar-keeper stared, and rubbed his chin thoughtfully. "Well, thar's that Kanaka Joe, who used to be sorter sweet on Mornie,--he's an ugly devil,--he's helpin' the old man."

The sad look faded from Ruth's eyes suddenly. A certain wild Berserker rage--a taint of the blood, inherited from heaven knows what Old-World ancestry, which had made the twin-brothers' Southwestern eccentricities respected in the settlement--glowed in its place. The barkeeper noted it, and augured a lively future for the day's festivities. But it faded again; and Ruth, as he rose, turned hesitatingly towards him.

"Have you seen my brother Rand lately?"

"Nary."

"He hasn't been here, or about the Ferry?"

"Nary time."

"You haven't heard," said Ruth, with a faint attempt at a smile, "if he's been around here asking after me,--sorter looking me up, you know?"

"Not much," returned the bar-keeper deliberately. "Ez far ez I know Rand,-- that ar brother o' yours,--he's one of yer high-toned chaps ez doesn't drink, thinks bar-rooms is pizen, and ain't the sort to come round yer, and sling yarns with me."

Ruth rose; but the hand that he placed upon the table, albeit a powerful one, trembled so that it was with difficulty he resumed his knapsack. When he did so, his bent figure, stooping shoulders, and haggard face, made him appear another man from the one who had sat down. There was a slight touch of apologetic defer- ence and humility in his manner as he paid his reckoning, and slowly and hesitat- ingly began to descend the steps.

The bar-keeper looked after him thoughtfully. "Well, dog my skin!" he ejacu- lated to himself, "ef I hadn't seen that man--that same Ruth Pinkney--straddle a friend's body in this yer very room, and dare a whole crowd to come on, I'd swar that he hadn't any grit in him. Thar's something up!"

But here Ruth reached the last step, and turned again.

"If you see old man Nixon, say I'm in town; if you see that -------- ----" (I re- gret to say that I cannot repeat his exact, and brief characterization of the present condition and natal antecedents of Kanaka Joe), "say I'm looking out for him," and was gone.

He wandered down the road, towards the one long, straggling street of the set- tlement. The few people who met him at that early hour greeted him with a kind of constrained civility; certain cautious souls hurried by without seeing him; all turned and looked after him; and a few followed him at a respectful distance. A somewhat notorious practical joker and recognized wag at the Ferry apparently awaited his coming with something of invitation and expectation, but, catching sight of Ruth's haggard face and blazing eyes, became instantly practical, and by no means jocular in his greeting. At the top of the hill, Ruth turned to look once more upon the dis- tant mountain, now again a mere cloud-line on the horizon. In the firm belief that he would never again see the sun rise upon it, he turned aside into a hazel-thicket, and, tearing out a few leaves from his pocket-book, wrote two letters,--one to Rand, and one to Mornie, but which, as they were never delivered, shall not burden this brief chronicle of that eventful day. For, while transcribing them, he was startled by the sounds of a dozen pistol-shots in the direction of the hotel he had recently quitted. Something in the mere sound provoked the old hereditary fighting instinct, and sent him to his feet with a bound, and a slight distension of the nostrils, and sniffing of the air, not unknown to certain men who become half intoxicated by the smell of powder. He quickly folded his letters, and addressed them carefully, and, taking off his knapsack and blanket, methodically arranged them under a tree, with the letters on top. Then he examined the lock of his revolver, and then, with the step of a man ten years younger, leaped into the road. He had scarcely done so when he was seized, and by sheer force dragged into a blacksmith's shop at the roadside. He turned his savage face and drawn weapon upon his assailant, but was surprised to meet the anxious eyes of the bar-keeper of the Mansion House.

"Don't be a d----d fool," said the man quickly. "Thar's fifty agin' you down thar. But why in h-ll didn't you wipe out old Nixon when you had such a good chance?"

"Wipe out old Nixon?" repeated Ruth.

"Yes; just now, when you had him covered."

"What!"

The bar-keeper turned quickly upon Ruth, stared at him, and then suddenly burst into a fit of laughter. "Well, I've knowed you two were twins, but damn me if I ever thought I'd be sold like this!" And he again burst into a roar of laughter.

"What do you mean?" demanded Ruth savagely.

"What do I mean?" returned the barkeeper. "Why, I mean this. I mean that your brother Rand, as you call him, he'z bin--for a young feller, and a pious feller--doin' about the tallest kind o' fightin' to-day that's been done at the Ferry. He laid out that ar Kanaka Joe and two of his chums. He was pitched into on your quarrel, and he took it up for you like a little man. I managed to drag him off, up yer in the hazel-bush for safety, and out you pops, and I thought you was him. He can't be far away. Halloo! There they're comin'; and thar's the doctor, trying to keep them back!"

A crowd of angry, excited faces, filled the road suddenly; but before them Dr. Duchesne, mounted, and with a pistol in his hand, opposed their further progress.

"Back in the bush!" whispered the barkeeper. "Now's your time!"

But Ruth stirred not. "Go you back," he said in a low voice, "find Rand, and take him away. I will fill his place here." He drew his revolver, and stepped into the road.

A shout, a report, and the spatter of red dust from a bullet near his feet, told him he was recognized. He stirred not; but another shout, and a cry, "There they are--BOTH of 'em!" made him turn.

His brother Rand, with a smile on his lip and fire in his eye, stood by his side. Neither spoke. Then Rand, quietly, as of old, slipped his hand into his brother's strong palm. Two or three bullets sang by them; a splinter flew from the blacksmith's shed: but the brothers, hard gripping each other's hands, and looking into each other's faces with a quiet joy, stood there calm and imperturbable.

There was a momentary pause. The voice of Dr. Duchesne rose above the crowd.

"Keep back, I say! keep back! Or hear me!--for five years I've worked among you, and mended and patched the holes you've drilled through each other's carcasses--Keep back, I say!--or the next man that pulls trigger, or steps forward, will get a hole from me that no surgeon can stop. I'm sick of your bungling ball practice! Keep back!--or, by the living Jingo, I'll show you where a man's vitals are!"

There was a burst of laughter from the crowd, and for a moment the twins were forgotten in this audacious speech and coolly impertinent presence.

"That's right! Now let that infernal old hypocritical drunkard, Mat Nixon, step to the front."

The crowd parted right and left, and half pushed, half dragged Nixon before him.

"Gentlemen," said the doctor, "this is the man who has just shot at Rand Pinkney for hiding his daughter. Now, I tell you, gentlemen, and I tell him, that for the last week his daughter, Mornie Nixon, has been under my care as a patient, and my protection as a friend. If there's anybody to be shot, the job must begin with me!"

There was another laugh, and a cry of "Bully for old Sawbones!" Ruth started convulsively, and Rand answered his look with a confirming pressure of his hand.

"That isn't all, gentlemen: this drunken brute has just shot at a gentleman whose only offence, to my knowledge, is, that he has, for the last week, treated her with a brother's kindness, has taken her into his own home, and cared for her wants as if she were his own sister."

Ruth's hand again grasped his brother's. Rand colored and hung his head.

"There's more yet, gentlemen. I tell you that that girl, Mornie Nixon, has, to my knowledge, been treated like a lady, has been cared for as she never was cared for in her father's house, and, while that father has been proclaiming her shame in every bar-room at the Ferry, has had the sympathy and care, night and day, of two of the most accomplished ladies of the Ferry,--Mrs. Sol Saunders, gentlemen, and Miss Euphemia."

There was a shout of approbation from the crowd. Nixon would have slipped away, but the doctor stopped him.

"Not yet! I've one thing more to say. I've to tell you, gentlemen, on my professional word of honor, that, besides being an old hypocrite, this same old Mat Nixon is the ungrateful, unnatural GRANDFATHER of the first boy born in the district."

A wild huzza greeted the doctor's climax. By a common consent the crowd turned toward the Twins, who, grasping each other's hands, stood apart. The doctor nodded his head. The next moment the Twins were surrounded, and lifted in the arms of the laughing throng, and borne in triumph to the bar-room of the Mansion House.

"Gentlemen," said the bar-keeper, "call for what you like: the Mansion House treats to-day in honor of its being the first time that Rand Pinkney has been admitted to the bar."

*****

It was agreed, that, as her condition was still precarious, the news should be broken to her gradually and indirectly. The indefatigable Sol had a professional idea, which was not displeasing to the Twins. It being a lovely summer afternoon, the couch of Mornie was lifted out on the ledge, and she lay there basking in the sunlight, drinking in the pure air, and looking bravely ahead in the daylight as she had in the darkness, for her couch commanded a view of the mountain flank. And, lying there, she dreamed a pleasant dream, and in her dream saw Rand returning up the mountain-trail. She was half conscious that he had good news for her; and, when he at last reached her bedside, he began gently and kindly to tell his news. But she heard him not, or rather in her dream was most occupied with his ways and manners, which seemed unlike him, yet inexpressibly sweet and tender. The tears were fast coming in her eyes, when he suddenly dropped on his knees beside her, threw away Rand's disguising hat and coat, and clasped her in his arms. And by that she KNEW it was Ruth.

But what they said; what hurried words of mutual explanation and forgiveness passed between them; what bitter yet tender recollections of hidden fears and doubts, now forever chased away in the rain of tears and joyous sunshine of that mountain-top, were then whispered; whatever of this little chronicle that to the reader seems strange and inconsistent (as all human record must ever be strange and imperfect, except to the actors) was then made clear,--was never divulged by them, and must remain with them forever. The rest of the party had withdrawn, and they were alone. But when Mornie turned, and placed the baby in its father's arms, they were so isolated in their happiness, that the lower world beneath them might have swung and drifted away, and left that mountain-top the beginning and creation of a better planet.

*****

"You know all about it now," said Sol the next day, explaining the previous episodes of this history to Ruth: "you've got the whole plot before you. It dragged a little in the second act, for the actors weren't up in their parts. But for an amateur performance, on the whole, it wasn't bad."

"I don't know, I'm sure," said Rand impulsively, "how we'd have got on without Euphemia. It's too bad she couldn't be here to-day."

"She wanted to come," said Sol; "but the gentleman she's engaged to came up from Marysville last night."

"Gentleman--engaged!" repeated Rand, white and red by turns.

"Well, yes. I say, 'gentleman,' although he's in the variety profession. She always said," said Sol, quietly looking at Rand, "that she'd never marry OUT of it."

AN HEIRESS OF RED DOG.

The first intimation given of the eccentricity of the testator was, I think, in the spring of 1854. He was at that time in possession of a considerable property, heavily mortgaged to one friend, and a wife of some attraction, on whose affections another friend held an encumbering lien. One day it was found that he had secretly dug, or caused to be dug, a deep trap before the front-door of his dwelling, into which a few friends, in the course of the evening, casually and familiarly dropped. This circumstance, slight in itself, seemed to point to the existence of a certain humor in the man, which might eventually get into literature, although his wife's lover-

-a man of quick discernment, whose leg was broken by the fall--took other views. It was some weeks later, that, while dining with certain other friends of his wife, he excused himself from the table to quietly re-appear at the front-window with a three-quarter inch hydraulic pipe, and a stream of water projected at the assembled company. An attempt was made to take public cognizance of this; but a majority of the citizens of Red Dog, who were not at dinner, decided that a man had a right to choose his own methods of diverting his company. Nevertheless, there were some hints of his insanity; his wife recalled other acts clearly attributable to dementia; the crippled lover argued from his own experience that the integrity of her limbs could only be secured by leaving her husband's house; and the mortgagee, fearing a further damage to his property, foreclosed. But here the cause of all this anxiety took matters into his own hands, and disappeared.

When we next heard from him, he had, in some mysterious way, been relieved alike of his wife and property, and was living alone at Rockville fifty miles away, and editing a newspaper. But that originality he had displayed when dealing with the problems of his own private life, when applied to politics in the columns of "The Rockville Vanguard" was singularly unsuccessful. An amusing exaggeration, purporting to be an exact account of the manner in which the opposing candidate had murdered his Chinese laundryman, was, I regret to say, answered only by assault and battery. A gratuitous and purely imaginative description of a great religious revival in Calaveras, in which the sheriff of the county--a notoriously profane sceptic--was alleged to have been the chief exhorter, resulted only in the withdrawal of the county advertising from the paper. In the midst of this practical confusion he suddenly died. It was then discovered, as a crowning proof of his absurdity, that he had left a will, bequeathing his entire effects to a freckle-faced maid-servant at the Rockville Hotel. But that absurdity became serious when it was also discovered that among these effects were a thousand shares in the Rising Sun Mining Company, which a day or two after his demise, and while people were still laughing at his grotesque benefaction, suddenly sprang into opulence and celebrity. Three millions of dollars was roughly estimated as the value of the estate thus wantonly sacrificed. For it is only fair to state, as a just tribute to the enterprise and energy of that young and thriving settlement, that there was not probably a single citizen who did not feel himself better able to control the deceased humorist's property. Some had expressed a doubt of their ability to support a family; others had felt perhaps too keenly the deep responsibility resting upon them when chosen from the panel as jurors, and had evaded their public duties; a few had declined office and a low salary: but no one shrank from the possibility of having been called upon to assume the functions of Peggy Moffat, the heiress.

The will was contested,--first by the widow, who it now appeared had never been legally divorced from the deceased; next by four of his cousins, who awoke, only too late, to a consciousness of his moral and pecuniary worth. But the humble legatee--a singularly plain, unpretending, uneducated Western girl--exhibited a dogged pertinacity in claiming her rights. She rejected all compromises. A rough sense of justice in the community, while doubting her ability to take care of the whole fortune, suggested that she ought to be content with three hundred thousand dollars. "She's bound to throw even THAT away on some derned skunk of a man, natoorally; but three millions is too much to give a chap for makin' her onhappy. It's offerin' a temptation to cussedness." The only opposing voice to this counsel came from the sardonic lips of Mr. Jack Hamlin. "Suppose," suggested that gentleman, turning abruptly on the speaker,--"suppose, when you won twenty thousand dollars of me last Friday night--suppose that, instead of handing you over the money as I did--suppose I'd got up on my hind-legs, and said, 'Look yer, Bill Wethersbee, you're a d----d fool. If I give ye that twenty thousand, you'll throw it away in the first skin-game in 'Frisco, and hand it over to the first short-card sharp you'll meet. There's a thousand,--enough for you to fling away,--take it and get!' Suppose what I'd said to you was the frozen truth, and you know'd it, would that have been the square thing to play on you?" But here Wethersbee quickly pointed out the inefficiency of the comparison by stating that HE had won the money fairly with a STAKE. "And how do you know," demanded Hamlin savagely, bending his black eyes on the astounded casuist,--"how do you know that the gal hezn't put down a stake?" The man stammered an unintelligible reply. The gambler laid his white hand on Wethersbee's shoulder. "Look yer, old man," he said, "every gal stakes her WHOLE pile,--you can bet your life on that,--whatever's her little game. If she took to keerds instead of her feelings, if she'd put up 'chips' instead o' body and soul, she'd bust every bank 'twixt this and 'Frisco! You hear me?"

Somewhat of this idea was conveyed, I fear not quite as sentimentally, to Peggy

Moffat herself. The best legal wisdom of San Francisco, retained by the widow and relatives, took occasion, in a private interview with Peggy, to point out that she stood in the quasi-criminal attitude of having unlawfully practised upon the affections of an insane elderly gentleman, with a view of getting possession of his property, and suggested to her that no vestige of her moral character would remain after the trial, if she persisted in forcing her claims to that issue. It is said that Peggy, on hearing this, stopped washing the plate she had in her hands, and, twisting the towel around her fingers, fixed her small pale blue eyes at the lawyer.

"And ez that the kind o' chirpin these critters keep up?"

"I regret to say, my dear young lady," responded the lawyer, "that the world is censorious. I must add," he continued, with engaging frankness, "that we professional lawyers are apt to study the opinion of the world, and that such will be the theory of--our side."

"Then," said Peggy stoutly, "ez I allow I've got to go into court to defend my character, I might as well pack in them three millions too."

There is hearsay evidence that Peg added to this speech a wish and desire to "bust the crust" of her traducers, and, remarking that "that was the kind of hairpin" she was, closed the conversation with an unfortunate accident to the plate, that left a severe contusion on the legal brow of her companion. But this story, popular in the bar-rooms and gulches, lacked confirmation in higher circles. Better authenticated was the legend related of an interview with her own lawyer. That gentleman had pointed out to her the advantage of being able to show some reasonable cause for the singular generosity of the testator.

"Although," he continued, "the law does not go back of the will for reason or cause for its provisions, it would be a strong point with the judge and jury--particularly if the theory of insanity were set up--for us to show that the act was logical and natural. Of course you have--I speak confidently, Miss Moffat--certain ideas of your own why the late Mr. Byways was so singularly generous to you."

"No, I haven't," said Peg decidedly.

"Think again. Had he not expressed to you--you understand that this is confidential between us, although I protest, my dear young lady, that I see no reason why it should not be made public--had he not given utterance to sentiments of a nature consistent with some future matrimonial relations?" But here Miss Peg's large mouth, which had been slowly relaxing over her irregular teeth, stopped him.

"If you mean he wanted to marry me--No!"

"I see. But were there any conditions--of course you know the law takes no cognizance of any not expressed in the will; but still, for the sake of mere corroboration of the bequest--do you know of any conditions on which he gave you the property?"

"You mean did he want anything in return?"

"Exactly, my dear young lady."

Peg's face on one side turned a deep magenta color, on the other a lighter cherry, while her nose was purple, and her forehead an Indian red. To add to the effect of this awkward and discomposing dramatic exhibition of embarrassment, she began to wipe her hands on her dress, and sat silent.

"I understand," said the lawyer hastily. "No matter--the conditions WERE fulfilled."

"No!" said Peg amazedly. "How could they be until he was dead?"

It was the lawyer's turn to color and grow embarrassed.

"He DID say something, and make some conditions," continued Peg, with a certain firmness through her awkwardness; "but that's nobody's business but mine and his'n. And it's no call o' yours or theirs."

"But, my dear Miss Moffat, if these very conditions were proofs of his right mind, you surely would not object to make them known, if only to enable you to put yourself in a condition to carry them out."

"But," said Peg cunningly, "s'pose you and the Court didn't think 'em satisfactory? S'pose you thought 'em QUEER? Eh?"

With this helpless limitation on the part of the defence, the case came to trial. Everybody remembers it,--how for six weeks it was the daily food of Calaveras County; how for six weeks the intellectual and moral and spiritual competency of Mr. James Byways to dispose of his property was discussed with learned and formal obscurity in the court, and with unlettered and independent prejudice by camp-fires and in bar-rooms. At the end of that time, when it was logically established that at least nine-tenths of the population of Calaveras were harmless lunatics, and everybody else's reason seemed to totter on its throne, an exhausted jury succumbed one day to the presence of Peg in the court-room. It was not a prepossessing presence at any time; but the excitement, and an injudicious attempt to ornament herself, brought her defects into a glaring relief that was almost unreal. Every freckle on her face stood out and asserted itself singly; her pale blue eyes, that gave no indication of her force of character, were weak and wandering, or stared blankly at the judge; her over-sized head, broad at the base, terminating in the scantiest possible light-colored braid in the middle of her narrow shoulders, was as hard and uninteresting as the wooden spheres that topped the railing against which she sat.

The jury, who for six weeks had had her described to them by the plaintiffs as an arch, wily enchantress, who had sapped the failing reason of Jim Byways, revolted to a man. There was something so appallingly gratuitous in her plainness, that it was felt that three millions was scarcely a compensation for it. "Ef that money was give to her, she earned it SURE, boys: it wasn't no softness of the old man," said the foreman. When the jury retired, it was felt that she had cleared her character: when they re-entered the room with their verdict, it was known that she had been awarded three millions damages for its defamation.

She got the money. But those who had confidently expected to see her squander it were disappointed: on the contrary, it was presently whispered that she was exceedingly penurious. That admirable woman, Mrs. Stiver of Red Dog, who accompanied her to San Francisco to assist her in making purchases, was loud in her indignation. "She cares more for two bits than I do for five dollars. She wouldn't buy anything at the 'City of Paris,' because it was 'too expensive,' and at last rigged herself out, a perfect guy, at some cheap slop-shops in Market Street. And after all the care Jane and me took of her, giving up our time and experience to her, she never so much as made Jane a single present." Popular opinion, which regarded Mrs. Stiver's attention as purely speculative, was not shocked at this unprofitable denouement; but when Peg refused to give anything to clear the mortgage off the new Presbyterian Church, and even declined to take shares in the Union Ditch, considered by many as an equally sacred and safe investment, she began to lose favor. Nevertheless, she seemed to be as regardless of public opinion as she had been before the trial; took a small house, in which she lived with an old woman who had once been a fellow-servant, on apparently terms of perfect equality, and looked after her money. I wish I could say that she did this discreetly; but the fact is, she blundered. The same dogged persistency she had displayed in claiming her rights was visible in her unsuccessful ventures. She sunk two hundred thousand dollars in a worn-out shaft originally projected by the deceased testator; she prolonged the miserable existence of "The Rockville Vanguard" long after it had ceased to interest even its enemies; she kept the doors of the Rockville Hotel open when its custom had departed; she lost the co-operation and favor of a fellow-capitalist through a trifling misunderstanding in which she was derelict and impenitent; she had three lawsuits on her hands that could have been settled for a trifle. I note these defects to show that she was by no means a heroine. I quote her affair with Jack Folinsbee to show she was scarcely the average woman.

That handsome, graceless vagabond had struck the outskirts of Red Dog in a cyclone of dissipation which left him a stranded but still rather interesting wreck in a ruinous cabin not far from Peg Moffat's virgin bower. Pale, crippled from excesses, with a voice quite tremulous from sympathetic emotion more or less developed by stimulants, he lingered languidly, with much time on his hands, and only a few neighbors. In this fascinating kind of general deshabille of morals, dress, and the emotions, he appeared before Peg Moffat. More than that, he occasionally limped with her through the settlement. The critical eye of Red Dog took in the singular pair,--Jack, voluble, suffering, apparently overcome by remorse, conscience, vituperation, and disease; and Peg, open-mouthed, high-colored, awkward, yet delighted; and the critical eye of Red Dog, seeing this, winked meaningly at Rockville. No one knew what passed between them; but all observed that one summer day Jack drove down the main street of Red Dog in an open buggy, with the heiress of that town beside him. Jack, albeit a trifle shaky, held the reins with something of his old dash; and Mistress Peggy, in an enormous bonnet with pearl-colored ribbons a shade darker than her hair, holding in her short, pink-gloved fingers a bouquet of yellow roses, absolutely glowed crimson in distressful gratification over the dashboard. So these two fared on, out of the busy settlement, into the woods, against the rosy sunset. Possibly it was not a pretty picture: nevertheless, as the dim aisles of the solemn pines opened to receive them, miners leaned upon their spades, and mechanics stopped in their toil to look after them. The critical eye of Red Dog, perhaps from the sun, perhaps from the fact that it had itself once been young and dissipated, took on a kindly moisture as it gazed.

The moon was high when they returned. Those who had waited to congratu-

late Jack on this near prospect of a favorable change in his fortunes were chagrined
to find, that, having seen the lady safe home, he had himself departed from Red
Dog. Nothing was to be gained from Peg, who, on the next day and ensuing days,
kept the even tenor of her way, sunk a thousand or two more in unsuccessful speculation, and made no change in her habits of personal economy. Weeks passed without any apparent sequel to this romantic idyl. Nothing was known definitely until
Jack, a month later, turned up in Sacramento, with a billiard-cue in his hand, and a
heart overcharged with indignant emotion. "I don't mind saying to you, gentlemen,
in confidence," said Jack to a circle of sympathizing players,--"I don't mind telling
you regarding this thing, that I was as soft on that freckled-faced, red-eyed, tallow-
haired gal, as if she'd been--a--a--an actress. And I don't mind saying, gentlemen,
that, as far as I understand women, she was just as soft on me. You kin laugh; but
it's so. One day I took her out buggy-riding,--in style, too,--and out on the road I offered to do the square thing, just as if she'd been a lady,--offered to marry her then
and there. And what did she do?" said Jack with a hysterical laugh. "Why, blank it
all! OFFERED ME TWENTY-FIVE DOLLARS A WEEK ALLOWANCE--PAY TO
BE STOPPED WHEN I WASN'T AT HOME!" The roar of laughter that greeted this
frank confession was broken by a quiet voice asking, "And what did YOU say?"--
"Say?" screamed Jack, "I just told her to go to ---- with her money."--"They say,"
continued the quiet voice, "that you asked her for the loan of two hundred and fifty
dollars to get you to Sacramento--and that you got it."--"Who says so roared Jack.
Show me the blank liar." There was a dead silence. Then the possessor of the quiet
voice, Mr. Jack Hamlin, languidly reached under the table, took the chalk, and,
rubbing the end of his billiard-cue, began with gentle gravity: "It was an old friend
of mine in Sacramento, a man with a wooden leg, a game eye, three fingers on his
right hand, and a consumptive cough. Being unable, naturally, to back himself, he
leaves things to me. So, for the sake of argument," continued Hamlin, suddenly laying down his cue, and fixing his wicked black eyes on the speaker, "say it's ME!"

I am afraid that this story, whether truthful or not, did not tend to increase
Peg's popularity in a community where recklessness and generosity condoned for
the absence of all the other virtues; and it is possible, also, that Red Dog was no more
free from prejudice than other more civilized but equally disappointed matchmak-
ers. Likewise, during the following year, she made several more foolish ventures,

and lost heavily. In fact, a feverish desire to increase her store at almost any risk seemed to possess her. At last it was announced that she intended to reopen the infelix Rockville Hotel, and keep it herself.

Wild as this scheme appeared in theory, when put into practical operation there seemed to be some chance of success. Much, doubtless, was owing to her practical knowledge of hotel-keeping, but more to her rigid economy and untiring industry. The mistress of millions, she cooked, washed, waited on table, made the beds, and labored like a common menial. Visitors were attracted by this novel spectacle. The income of the house increased as their respect for the hostess lessened. No anecdote of her avarice was too extravagant for current belief. It was even alleged that she had been known to carry the luggage of guests to their rooms, that she might antici-pate the usual porter's gratuity. She denied herself the ordinary necessaries of life. She was poorly clad, she was ill-fed--but the hotel was making money.

A few hinted of insanity; others shook their heads, and said a curse was en-tailed on the property. It was believed, also, from her appearance, that she could not long survive this tax on her energies, and already there was discussion as to the probable final disposition of her property.

It was the particular fortune of Mr. Jack Hamlin to be able to set the world right on this and other questions regarding her.

A stormy December evening had set in when he chanced to be a guest of the Rockville Hotel. He had, during the past week, been engaged in the prosecution of his noble profession at Red Dog, and had, in the graphic language of a coadjutor, "cleared out the town, except his fare in the pockets of the stage-driver." "The Red Dog Standard" had bewailed his departure in playful obituary verse, beginning, "Dearest Johnny, thou hast left us," wherein the rhymes "bereft us" and "deplore" carried a vague allusion to "a thousand dollars more." A quiet contentment natu-rally suffused his personality, and he was more than usually lazy and deliberate in his speech. At midnight, when he was about to retire, he was a little surprised, how-ever, by a tap on his door, followed by the presence of Mistress Peg Moffat, heiress, and landlady of Rockville hotel.

Mr. Hamlin, despite his previous defence of Peg, had no liking for her. His fastidious taste rejected her uncomeliness; his habits of thought and life were all antagonistic to what he had heard of her niggardliness and greed. As she stood there, in a dirty calico wrapper, still redolent with the day's cuisine, crimson with embarrassment and the recent heat of the kitchen range, she certainly was not an alluring apparition. Happily for the lateness of the hour, her loneliness, and the infelix reputation of the man before her, she was at least a safe one. And I fear the very consciousness of this scarcely relieved her embarrassment.

"I wanted to say a few words to ye alone, Mr. Hamlin," she began, taking an unoffered seat on the end of his portmanteau, "or I shouldn't hev intruded. But it's the only time I can ketch you, or you me; for I'm down in the kitchen from sunup till now."

She stopped awkwardly, as if to listen to the wind, which was rattling the windows, and spreading a film of rain against the opaque darkness without. Then, smoothing her wrapper over her knees, she remarked, as if opening a desultory conversation, "Thar's a power of rain outside."

Mr. Hamlin's only response to this meteorological observation was a yawn, and a preliminary tug at his coat as he began to remove it.

"I thought ye couldn't mind doin' me a favor," continued Peg, with a hard, awkward laugh, "partik'ly seein' ez folks allowed you'd sorter bin a friend o' mine, and hed stood up for me at times when you hedn't any partikler call to do it. I hevn't" she continued, looking down on her lap, and following with her finger and thumb a seam of her gown,--"I hevn't so many friends ez slings a kind word for me these times that I disremember them." Her under lip quivered a little here; and, after vainly hunting for a forgotten handkerchief, she finally lifted the hem of her gown, wiped her snub nose upon it, but left the tears still in her eyes as she raised them to the man, Mr. Hamlin, who had by this time divested himself of his coat, stopped unbuttoning his waistcoat, and looked at her.

"Like ez not thar'll be high water on the North Fork, ef this rain keeps on," said Peg, as if apologetically, looking toward the window.

The other rain having ceased, Mr. Hamlin began to unbutton his waistcoat again.

"I wanted to ask ye a favor about Mr.--about--Jack Folinsbee," began Peg again hurriedly. "He's ailin' agin, and is mighty low. And he's losin' a heap o' money here and thar, and mostly to YOU. You cleaned him out of two thousand dollars last night--all he had."

"Well?" said the gambler coldly.

"Well, I thought ez you woz a friend o' mine, I'd ask ye to let up a little on him," said Peg, with an affected laugh. "You kin do it. Don't let him play with ye."

"Mistress Margaret Moffat," said Jack, with lazy deliberation, taking off his watch, and beginning to wind it up, "ef you're that much stuck after Jack Folinsbee, YOU kin keep him off of me much easier than I kin. You're a rich woman. Give him enough money to break my bank, or break himself for good and all; but don't keep him forlin' round me in hopes to make a raise. It don't pay, Mistress Moffat--it don't pay!"

A finer nature than Peg's would have misunderstood or resented the gambler's slang, and the miserable truths that underlaid it. But she comprehended him instantly, and sat hopelessly silent.

"Ef you'll take my advice," continued Jack, placing his watch and chain under his pillow, and quietly unloosing his cravat, "you'll quit this yer forlin', marry that chap, and hand over to him the money and the money-makin' that's killin' you. He'll get rid of it soon enough. I don't say this because I expect to git it; for, when he's got that much of a raise, he'll make a break for 'Frisco, and lose it to some first-class sport THERE. I don't say, neither, that you mayn't be in luck enough to reform him. I don't say, neither--and it's a derned sight more likely!--that you mayn't be luckier yet, and he'll up and die afore he gits rid of your money. But I do say you'll make him happy NOW; and, ez I reckon you're about ez badly stuck after that chap ez I ever saw any woman, you won't be hurtin' your own feelin's either."

The blood left Peg's face as she looked up. "But that's WHY I can't give him the money--and he won't marry me without it."

Mr. Hamlin's hand dropped from the last button of his waistcoat. "Can't--give--him--the--money?" he repeated slowly.

"No."

"Why?"

"Because--because I LOVE him."

Mr. Hamlin rebuttoned his waistcoat, and sat down patiently on the bed. Peg arose, and awkwardly drew the portmanteau a little nearer to him.

"When Jim Byways left me this yer property," she began, looking cautiously around, "he left it to me on CONDITIONS; not conditions ez waz in his WRITTEN will, but conditions ez waz SPOKEN. A promise I made him in this very room, Mr. Hamlin,--this very room, and on that very bed you're sittin' on, in which he died."

Like most gamblers, Mr. Hamlin was superstitious. He rose hastily from the bed, and took a chair beside the window. The wind shook it as if the discontented spirit of Mr. Byways were without, re-enforcing his last injunction.

"I don't know if you remember him," said Peg feverishly, "he was a man ez hed suffered. All that he loved--wife, fammerly, friends--had gone back on him. He tried to make light of it afore folks; but with me, being a poor gal, he let himself out. I never told anybody this. I don't know why he told ME; I don't know," continued Peg, with a sniffle, "why he wanted to make me unhappy too. But he made me promise, that, if he left me his fortune, I'd NEVER, NEVER--so help me God!--never share it with any man or woman that I LOVED; I didn't think it would be hard to keep that promise then, Mr. Hamlin; for I was very poor, and hedn't a friend nor a living bein' that was kind to me, but HIM."

"But you've as good as broken your promise already," said Hamlin. "You've given Jack money, as I know."

"Only what I made myself. Listen to me, Mr. Hamlin. When Jack proposed to me, I offered him about what I kalkilated I could earn myself. When he went away, and was sick and in trouble, I came here and took this hotel. I knew that by hard work I could make it pay. Don't laugh at me, please. I DID work hard, and DID make it pay--without takin' one cent of the fortin'. And all I made, workin' by night and day, I gave to him. I did, Mr. Hamlin. I ain't so hard to him as you think, though I might be kinder, I know."

Mr. Hamlin rose, deliberately resumed his coat, watch, hat, and overcoat. When he was completely dressed again, he turned to Peg. "Do you mean to say that you've been givin' all the money you made here to this A 1 first-class cherubim?"

"Yes; but he didn't know where I got it. O Mr. Hamlin! he didn't know that."

"Do I understand you, that he's bin buckin agin Faro with the money that you raised on hash? And YOU makin' the hash?"

"But he didn't know that, he wouldn't hev took it if I'd told him."

"No, he'd hev died fust!" said Mr. Hamlin gravely. "Why, he's that sensitive--is Jack Folinsbee--that it nearly kills him to take money even of ME. But where does this angel reside when he isn't fightin' the tiger, and is, so to speak, visible to the naked eye?"

"He--he--stops here," said Peg, with an awkward blush.

"I see. Might I ask the number of his room--or should I be a--disturbing him in his meditations?" continued Jack Hamlin, with grave politeness.

"Oh! then you'll promise? And you'll talk to him, and make HIM promise?"

"Of course," said Hamlin quietly.

"And you'll remember he's sick--very sick? His room's No. 44, at the end of the hall. Perhaps I'd better go with you?"

"I'll find it."

"And you won't be too hard on him?"

"I'll be a father to him," said Hamlin demurely, as he opened the door and stepped into the hall. But he hesitated a moment, and then turned, and gravely held out his hand. Peg took it timidly. He did not seem quite in earnest; and his black eyes, vainly questioned, indicated nothing. But he shook her hand warmly, and the next moment was gone.

He found the room with no difficulty. A faint cough from within, and a querulous protest, answered his knock. Mr. Hamlin entered without further ceremony. A sickening smell of drugs, a palpable flavor of stale dissipation, and the wasted figure of Jack Folinsbee, half-dressed, extended upon the bed, greeted him. Mr. Hamlin was for an instant startled. There were hollow circles round the sick man's eyes; there was palsy in his trembling limbs; there was dissolution in his feverish breath.

"What's up?" he asked huskily and nervously.

"I am, and I want YOU to get up too."

"I can't, Jack. I'm regularly done up." He reached his shaking hand towards a glass half-filled with suspicious, pungent-smelling liquid; but Mr. Hamlin stayed it.

"Do you want to get back that two thousand dollars you lost?"

"Yes."

"Well, get up, and marry that woman down stairs."

Folinsbee laughed half hysterically, half sardonically.

"She won't give it to me."

"No; but I will."

"YOU?"

"Yes."

Folinsbee, with an attempt at a reckless laugh, rose, trembling and with difficulty, to his swollen feet. Hamlin eyed him narrowly, and then bade him lie down again. "To-morrow will do," he said, "and then--"

"If I don't--"

"If you don't," responded Hamlin, "why, I'll just wade in and CUT YOU OUT!"

But on the morrow Mr. Hamlin was spared that possible act of disloyalty; for, in the night, the already hesitating spirit of Mr. Jack Folinsbee took flight on the wings of the south-east storm. When or how it happened, nobody knew. Whether this last excitement and the near prospect of matrimony, or whether an overdose of anodyne, had hastened his end, was never known. I only know, that, when they came to awaken him the next morning, the best that was left of him--a face still beautiful and boy-like--looked up coldly at the tearful eyes of Peg Moffat. "It serves me right, it's a judgment," she said in a low whisper to Jack Hamlin; "for God knew that I'd broken my word, and willed all my property to him."

She did not long survive him. Whether Mr. Hamlin ever clothed with action the suggestion indicated in his speech to the lamented Jack that night, is not of record. He was always her friend, and on her demise became her executor. But the bulk of her property was left to a distant relation of handsome Jack Folinsbee, and so passed out of the control of Red Dog forever.

THE GREAT DEADWOOD MYSTERY

It was growing quite dark in the telegraph-office at Cottonwood, Tuolumne County, California. The office, a box-like enclosure, was separated from the public room of the Miners' Hotel by a thin partition; and the operator, who was also news and express agent at Cottonwood, had closed his window, and was lounging by his news-stand preparatory to going home. Without, the first monotonous rain of the season was dripping from the porches of the hotel in the waning light of a December day. The operator, accustomed as he was to long intervals of idleness, was fast becoming bored.

The tread of mud-muffled boots on the veranda, and the entrance of two men, offered a momentary excitement. He recognized in the strangers two prominent citizens of Cottonwood; and their manner bespoke business. One of them proceeded to the desk, wrote a despatch, and handed it to the other interrogatively.

"That's about the way the thing p'ints," responded his companion assentingly.

"I reckoned it only squar to use his diential words?"

"That's so."

The first speaker turned to the operator with the despatch.

"How soon can you shove her through?"

The operator glanced professionally over the address and the length of the despatch.

"Now," he answered promptly.

"And she gets there?"

"To-night. But there's no delivery until to-morrow."

"Shove her through to-night, and say there's an extra twenty left here for delivery."

The operator, accustomed to all kinds of extravagant outlay for expedition, replied that he would lay this proposition with the despatch, before the San Francisco office. He then took it and read it--and re-read it. He preserved the usual professional apathy,--had doubtless sent many more enigmatical and mysterious messages,--but nevertheless, when he finished, he raised his eyes inquiringly to his customer. That gentleman, who enjoyed a reputation for equal spontaneity of temper and revolver, met his gaze a little impatiently. The operator had recourse to a trick. Under the pretence of misunderstanding the message, he obliged the sender to repeat it aloud for the sake of accuracy, and even suggested a few verbal alterations, ostensibly to insure correctness, but really to extract further information. Nevertheless, the man doggedly persisted in a literal transcript of his message. The operator went to his instrument hesitatingly.

"I suppose," he added half-questioningly, "there ain't no chance of a mistake. This address is Rightbody, that rich old Bostonian that everybody knows. There ain't but one?"

"That's the address," responded the first speaker coolly.

"Didn't know the old chap had investments out here," suggested the operator, lingering at his instrument.

"No more did I," was the insufficient reply.

For some few moments nothing was heard but the click of the instrument, as the operator worked the key, with the usual appearance of imparting confidence to a somewhat reluctant hearer who preferred to talk himself. The two men stood by, watching his motions with the usual awe of the unprofessional. When he had finished, they laid before him two gold-pieces. As the operator took them up, he could not help saying,--

"The old man went off kinder sudden, didn't he? Had no time to write?"

"Not sudden for that kind o' man," was the exasperating reply.

But the speaker was not to be disconcerted. "If there is an answer--" he began.

"There ain't any," replied the first speaker quietly.

"Why?"

"Because the man ez sent the message is dead."

"But it's signed by you two."

"On'y ez witnesses--eh?" appealed the first speaker to his comrade.

"On'y ez witnesses," responded the other.

The operator shrugged his shoulders. The business concluded, the first speaker slightly relaxed. He nodded to the operator, and turned to the bar-room with a pleasing social impulse. When their glasses were set down empty, the first speaker, with a cheerful condemnation of the hard times and the weather, apparently dismissed all previous proceedings from his mind, and lounged out with his companion. At the corner of the street they stopped.

"Well, that job's done," said the first speaker, by way of relieving the slight social embarrassment of parting.

"Thet's so," responded his companion, and shook his hand.

They parted. A gust of wind swept through the pines, and struck a faint Aeolian cry from the wires above their heads; and the rain and the darkness again slowly settled upon Cottonwood.

The message lagged a little at San Francisco, laid over half an hour at Chicago, and fought longitude the whole way; so that it was past midnight when the "all night" operator took it from the wires at Boston. But it was freighted with a mandate from the San Francisco office; and a messenger was procured, who sped with it through dark snow-bound streets, between the high walls of close-shuttered rayless houses, to a certain formal square ghostly with snow-covered statues. Here he ascended the broad steps of a reserved and solid-looking mansion, and pulled a bronze bell-knob, that somewhere within those chaste recesses, after an apparent reflective pause, coldly communicated the fact that a stranger was waiting without--as he ought. Despite the lateness of the hour, there was a slight glow from the windows, clearly not enough to warm the messenger with indications of a festivity within, but yet bespeaking, as it were, some prolonged though subdued excitement. The sober servant who took the despatch, and receipted for it as gravely as if witnessing a last will and testament, respectfully paused before the entrance of the drawing-room. The sound of measured and rhetorical speech, through which the occasional catarrhal cough of the New-England coast struggled, as the only effort of nature not wholly repressed, came from its heavily-curtained recesses; for the occasion of the evening had been the reception and entertainment of various distinguished persons, and, as had been epigrammatically expressed by one of the guests, "the history of the country" was taking its leave in phrases more or less memorable and characteristic. Some of these valedictory axioms were clever, some witty, a few profound, but always left as a genteel contribution to the entertainer. Some had been already prepared, and, like a card, had served and identified the guest at other mansions.

The last guest departed, the last carriage rolled away, when the servant ventured to indicate the existence of the despatch to his master, who was standing on the hearth-rug in an attitude of wearied self-righteousness. He took it, opened it, read it, re-read it, and said,--

"There must be some mistake! It is not for me. Call the boy, Waters."

Waters, who was perfectly aware that the boy had left, nevertheless obediently walked towards the hall-door, but was recalled by his master.

"No matter--at present!"

"It's nothing serious, William?" asked Mrs. Rightbody, with languid wifely concern.

"No, nothing. Is there a light in my study?"

"Yes. But, before you go, can you give me a moment or two?"

Mr. Rightbody turned a little impatiently towards his wife. She had thrown herself languidly on the sofa; her hair was slightly disarranged, and part of a slippered foot was visible. She might have been a finely-formed woman; but even her careless deshabille left the general impression that she was severely flannelled throughout, and that any ostentation of womanly charm was under vigorous sanitary SURVEILLANCE.

"Mrs. Marvin told me to-night that her son made no secret of his serious attachment for our Alice, and that, if I was satisfied, Mr. Marvin would be glad to confer with you at once."

The information did not seem to absorb Mr. Rightbody's wandering attention, but rather increased his impatience. He said hastily, that he would speak of that to-morrow; and partly by way of reprisal, and partly to dismiss the subject, added--

"Positively James must pay some attention to the register and the thermometer. It was over 70 degrees to-night, and the ventilating draught was closed in the drawing-room."

"That was because Professor Ammon sat near it, and the old gentleman's tonsils are so sensitive."

"He ought to know from Dr. Dyer Doit that systematic and regular exposure to draughts stimulates the mucous membrane; while fixed air over 60 degrees invariably--"

"I am afraid, William," interrupted Mrs. Rightbody, with feminine adroitness, adopting her husband's topic with a view of thereby directing him from it,--"I'm afraid that people do not yet appreciate the substitution of bouillon for punch and ices. I observed that Mr. Spondee declined it, and, I fancied, looked disappointed. The fibrine and wheat in liqueur-glasses passed quite unnoticed too."

"And yet each half-drachm contained the half-digested substance of a pound of beef. I'm surprised at Spondee!" continued Mr. Rightbody aggrievedly. "Exhausting his brain and nerve force by the highest creative efforts of the Muse, he prefers perfumed and diluted alcohol flavored with carbonic acid gas. Even Mrs. Faringway admitted to me that the sudden lowering of the temperature of the stomach by the introduction of ice--"

"Yes; but she took a lemon ice at the last Dorothea Reception, and asked me if I had observed that the lower animals refused their food at a temperature over 60 degrees."

Mr. Rightbody again moved impatiently towards the door. Mrs. Rightbody eyed him curiously.

"You will not write, I hope? Dr. Keppler told me to-night that your cerebral symptoms interdicted any prolonged mental strain."

"I must consult a few papers," responded Mr. Rightbody curtly, as he entered his library.

It was a richly-furnished apartment, morbidly severe in its decorations, which were symptomatic of a gloomy dyspepsia of art, then quite prevalent. A few curios, very ugly, but providentially equally rare, were scattered about. There were various bronzes, marbles, and casts, all requiring explanation, and so fulfilling their purpose of promoting conversation, and exhibiting the erudition of their owner. There were souvenirs of travel with a history, old bric-a-brac with a pedigree, but little or nothing that challenged attention for itself alone. In all cases the superiority of the owner to his possessions was admitted. As a natural result, nobody ever lingered there, the servants avoided the room, and no child was ever known to play in it.

Mr. Rightbody turned up the gas, and from a cabinet of drawers, precisely labelled, drew a package of letters. These he carefully examined. All were discolored, and made dignified by age; but some, in their original freshness, must have appeared trifling, and inconsistent with any correspondent of Mr. Rightbody. Nevertheless, that gentleman spent some moments in carefully perusing them, occasionally referring to the telegram in his hand. Suddenly there was a knock at the door. Mr. Rightbody started, made a half-unconscious movement to return the letters to the drawer, turned the telegram face downwards, and then, somewhat harshly, stammered,--

"Eh? Who's there? Come in."

"I beg your pardon, papa," said a very pretty girl, entering, without, however, the slightest trace of apology or awe in her manner, and taking a chair with the self-possession and familiarity of an habitue of the room; "but I knew it was not your habit to write late, so I supposed you were not busy. I am on my way to bed."

She was so very pretty, and withal so utterly unconscious of it, or perhaps so consciously superior to it, that one was provoked into a more critical examination of her face. But this only resulted in a reiteration of her beauty, and perhaps the added facts that her dark eyes were very womanly, her rich complexion eloquent, and her chiselled lips fell enough to be passionate or capricious, notwithstanding that their general effect suggested neither caprice, womanly weakness, nor passion.

With the instinct of an embarrassed man, Mr. Rightbody touched the topic he would have preferred to avoid.

"I suppose we must talk over to-morrow," he hesitated, "this matter of yours and Mr. Marvin's? Mrs. Marvin has formally spoken to your mother."

Miss Alice lifted her bright eyes intelligently, but not joyfully; and the color of action, rather than embarrassment, rose to her round cheeks.

"Yes, HE said she would," she answered simply.

"At present," continued Mr. Rightbody still awkwardly, "I see no objection to the proposed arrangement."

Miss Alice opened her round eyes at this.

"Why, papa, I thought it had been all settled long ago! Mamma knew it, you knew it. Last July, mamma and you talked it over."

"Yes, yes," returned her father, fumbling his papers; "that is--well, we will talk of it to-morrow." In fact, Mr. Rightbody HAD intended to give the affair a proper attitude of seriousness and solemnity by due precision of speech, and some apposite reflections, when he should impart the news to his daughter, but felt himself unable to do it now. "I am glad, Alice," he said at last, "that you have quite forgotten your previous whims and fancies. You see WE are right."

"Oh! I dare say, papa, if I'm to be married at all, that Mr. Marvin is in every way suitable."

Mr. Rightbody looked at his daughter narrowly. There was not the slightest impatience nor bitterness in her manner: it was as well regulated as the sentiment she expressed.

"Mr. Marvin is--" he began.

"I know what Mr. Marvin IS," interrupted Miss Alice; "and he has promised me that I shall be allowed to go on with my studies the same as before. I shall graduate with my class; and, if I prefer to practise my profession, I can do so in two years after our marriage."

"In two years?" queried Mr. Rightbody curiously.

"Yes. You see, in case we should have a child, that would give me time enough to wean it."

Mr. Rightbody looked at this flesh of his flesh, pretty and palpable flesh as it was; but, being confronted as equally with the brain of his brain, all he could do was to say meekly,--

"Yes, certainly. We will see about all that to-morrow."

Miss Alice rose. Something in the free, unfettered swing of her arms as she rested them lightly, after a half yawn, on her lithe hips, suggested his next speech, although still distrait and impatient.

"You continue your exercise with the health-lift yet, I see."

"Yes, papa; but I had to give up the flannels. I don't see how mamma could wear them. But my dresses are high-necked, and by bathing I toughen my skin. See!" she added, as, with a child-like unconsciousness, she unfastened two or three buttons of her gown, and exposed the white surface of her throat and neck to her father, "I can defy a chill."

Mr. Rightbody, with something akin to a genuine playful, paternal laugh, leaned forward and kissed her forehead.

"It's getting late, Ally," he said parentally, but not dictatorially. "Go to bed."

"I took a nap of three hours this afternoon," said Miss Alice, with a dazzling smile, "to anticipate this dissipation. Good-night, papa. To-morrow, then."

"To-morrow," repeated Mr. Rightbody, with his eyes still fixed upon the girl vaguely. "Good-night."

Miss Alice tripped from the room, possibly a trifle the more light-heartedly that she had parted from her father in one of his rare moments of illogical human weakness. And perhaps it was well for the poor girl that she kept this single remembrance of him, when, I fear, in after-years, his methods, his reasoning, and indeed all he had tried to impress upon her childhood, had faded from her memory.

For, when she had left, Mr. Rightbody fell again to the examination of his old letters. This was quite absorbing; so much so, that he did not notice the footsteps of Mrs. Rightbody, on the staircase as she passed to her chamber, nor that she had paused on the landing to look through the glass half-door on her husband, as he sat there with the letters beside him, and the telegram opened before him. Had she waited a moment later, she would have seen him rise, and walk to the sofa with a disturbed air and a slight confusion; so that, on reaching it, he seemed to hesitate to lie down, although pale and evidently faint. Had she still waited, she would have seen him rise again with an agonized effort, stagger to the table, fumblingly refold and replace the papers in the cabinet, and lock it, and, although now but half-conscious, hold the telegram over the gas-flame till it was consumed.

For, had she waited until this moment, she would have flown unhesitatingly to his aid, as, this act completed, he staggered again, reached his hand toward the bell, but vainly, and then fell prone upon the sofa.

But alas! no providential nor accidental hand was raised to save him, or antici-pate the progress of this story. And when, half an hour later, Mrs. Rightbody, a little alarmed, and more indignant at his violation of the doctor's rules, appeared upon the threshold, Mr. Rightbody lay upon the sofa, dead!

With bustle, with thronging feet, with the irruption of strangers, and a hur-rying to and fro, but, more than all, with an impulse and emotion unknown to the mansion when its owner was in life, Mrs. Rightbody strove to call back the vanished life, but in vain. The highest medical intelligence, called from its bed at this strange hour, saw only the demonstration of its theories made a year before. Mr. Rightbody was dead--without doubt, without mystery, even as a correct man should die--logically, and indorsed by the highest medical authority.

But even in the confusion, Mrs. Rightbody managed to speed a messenger to the telegraph-office for a copy of the despatch received by Mr. Rightbody, but now missing.

In the solitude of her own room, and without a confidant, she read these words:--

    "[Copy.]
    "To MR. ADAMS RIGHTBODY, BOSTON, MASS.
    "Joshua Silsbie died suddenly this morning. His last request was
      that you should remember your sacred compact with him of thirty
    years ago. "SEVENTY-FOUR. "SEVENTY-FIVE."

In the darkened home, and amid the formal condolements of their friends who had called to gaze upon the scarcely cold features of their late associate, Mrs. Right-body managed to send another despatch. It was addressed to "Seventy-Four and Seventy-Five," Cottonwood. In a few hours she received the following enigmatical response:--

"A horse-thief named Josh Silsbie was lynched yesterday morning by the Vigi-lantes at Deadwood."

PART II.

The spring of 1874 was retarded in the California sierras; so much so, that certain Eastern tourists who had early ventured into the Yo Semite Valley found themselves, one May morning, snow-bound against the tempestuous shoulders of El Capitan. So furious was the onset of the wind at the Upper Merced Canyon, that even so respectable a lady as Mrs. Rightbody was fain to cling to the neck of her guide to keep her seat in the saddle; while Miss Alice, scorning all masculine assistance, was hurled, a lovely chaos, against the snowy wall of the chasm. Mrs. Rightbody screamed; Miss Alice raged under her breath, but scrambled to her feet again in silence.

"I told you so!" said Mrs. Rightbody, in an indignant whisper, as her daughter again ranged beside her. "I warned you especially, Alice--that--that--"

"What?" interrupted Miss Alice curtly.

"That you would need your chemiloons and high boots," said Mrs. Rightbody, in a regretful undertone, slightly increasing her distance from the guides.

Miss Alice shrugged her pretty shoulders scornfully, but ignored her mother's implication.

"You were particularly warned against going into the valley at this season," she only replied grimly.

Mrs. Rightbody raised her eyes impatiently.

"You know how anxious I was to discover your poor father's strange correspondent, Alice. You have no consideration."

"But when YOU HAVE discovered him--what then?" queried Miss Alice.

"What then?"

"Yes. My belief is, that you will find the telegram only a mere business cipher, and all this quest mere nonsense."

"Alice! Why, YOU yourself thought your father's conduct that night very strange. Have you forgotten?"

The young lady had NOT, but, for some far-reaching feminine reason, chose to ignore it at that moment, when her late tumble in the snow was still fresh in her mind.

"And this woman, whoever she may be--" continued Mrs. Rightbody.

"How do you know there's a woman in the case?" interrupted Miss Alice, wickedly I fear.

"How do--I--know--there's a woman?" slowly ejaculated Mrs. Rightbody, floundering in the snow and the unexpected possibility of such a ridiculous question. But here her guide flew to her assistance, and estopped further speech. And, indeed, a grave problem was before them.

The road that led to their single place of refuge--a cabin, half hotel, half trading-post, scarce a mile away--skirted the base of the rocky dome, and passed perilously near the precipitous wall of the valley. There was a rapid descent of a hundred yards or more to this terrace-like passage; and the guides paused for a moment of consultation, cooly oblivious, alike to the terrified questioning of Mrs. Rightbody, or the half-insolent independence of the daughter. The elder guide was russet-bearded, stout, and humorous: the younger was dark-bearded, slight, and serious.

"Ef you kin git young Bunker Hill to let you tote her on your shoulders, I'll git the Madam to hang on to me," came to Mrs. Rightbody's horrified ears as the expression of her particular companion.

"Freeze to the old gal, and don't reckon on me if the daughter starts in to play it alone," was the enigmatical response of the younger guide.

Miss Alice overheard both propositions; and, before the two men returned to their side, that high-spirited young lady had urged her horse down the declivity.

Alas! at this moment a gust of whirling snow swept down upon her. There was a flounder, a mis-step, a fatal strain on the wrong rein, a fall, a few plucky but unavailing struggles, and both horse and rider slid ignominiously down toward the rocky shelf. Mrs. Rightbody screamed. Miss Alice, from a confused debris of snow and ice, uplifted a vexed and coloring face to the younger guide, a little the more angrily, perhaps, that she saw a shade of impatience on his face.

"Don't move, but tie one end of the 'lass' under your arms, and throw me the other," he said quietly.

"What do you mean by 'lass'--the lasso?" asked Miss Alice disgustedly.

"Yes, ma'am."

"Then why don't you say so?"

"O Alice!" reproachfully interpolated Mrs. Rightbody, encircled by the elder guide's stalwart arm.

Miss Alice deigned no reply, but drew the loop of the lasso over her shoulders, and let it drop to her round waist. Then she essayed to throw the other end to her guide. Dismal failure! The first fling nearly knocked her off the ledge; the second went all wild against the rocky wall; the third caught in a thorn-bush, twenty feet below her companion's feet. Miss Alice's arm sunk helplessly to her side, at which signal of unqualified surrender, the younger guide threw himself half way down the slope, worked his way to the thorn-bush, hung for a moment perilously over the parapet, secured the lasso, and then began to pull away at his lovely burden. Miss Alice was no dead weight, however, but steadily half-scrambled on her hands and knees to within a foot or two of her rescuer. At this too familiar proximity, she stood up, and leaned a little stiffly against the line, causing the guide to give an extra pull, which had the lamentable effect of landing her almost in his arms.

As it was, her intelligent forehead struck his nose sharply, and I regret to add, treating of a romantic situation, caused that somewhat prominent sign and token of a hero to bleed freely. Miss Alice instantly clapped a handful of snow over his nostrils.

"Now elevate your right arm," she said commandingly.

He did as he was bidden, but sulkily.

"That compresses the artery."

No man, with a pretty woman's hand and a handful of snow over his mouth and nose, could effectively utter a heroic sentence, nor, with his arm elevated stiffly over his head, assume a heroic attitude. But, when his mouth was free again, he said half-sulkily, half-apologetically,--

"I might have known a girl couldn't throw worth a cent."

"Why?" demanded Miss Alice sharply.

"Because--why--because--you see--they haven't got the experience," he stammered feebly.

"Nonsense! they haven't the CLAVICLE--that's all! It's because I'm a woman, and smaller in the collar-bone, that I haven't the play of the fore-arm which you have. See!" She squared her shoulders slightly, and turned the blaze of her dark eyes full on his. "Experience, indeed! A girl can learn anything a boy can."

Apprehension took the place of ill-humor in her hearer. He turned his eyes hastily away, and glanced above him. The elder guide had gone forward to catch Miss Alice's horse, which, relieved of his rider, was floundering toward the trail. Mrs. Rightbody was nowhere to be seen. And these two were still twenty feet below the trail!

There was an awkward pause.

"Shall I put you up the same way?" he queried. Miss Alice looked at his nose, and hesitated. "Or will you take my hand?" he added in surly impatience. To his surprise, Miss Alice took his hand, and they began the ascent together.

But the way was difficult and dangerous. Once or twice her feet slipped on the smoothly-worn rock beneath; and she confessed to an inward thankfulness when her uncertain feminine hand-grip was exchanged for his strong arm around her waist. Not that he was ungentle; but Miss Alice angrily felt that he had once or twice exercised his superior masculine functions in a rough way; and yet the next moment she would have probably rejected the idea that she had even noticed it. There was no doubt, however, that he WAS a little surly.

A fierce scramble finally brought them back in safety to the trail; but in the action Miss Alice's shoulder, striking a projecting bowlder, wrung from her a feminine cry of pain, her first sign of womanly weakness. The guide stopped instantly.

"I am afraid I hurt you?"

She raised her brown lashes, a trifle moist from suffering, looked in his eyes, and dropped her own. Why, she could not tell. And yet he had certainly a kind face, despite its seriousness; and a fine face, albeit unshorn and weather-beaten. Her own eyes had never been so near to any man's before, save her lover's; and yet she had never seen so much in even his. She slipped her hand away, not with any reference to him, but rather to ponder over this singular experience, and somehow felt uncomfortable thereat.

Nor was he less so. It was but a few days ago that he had accepted the charge of this young woman from the elder guide, who was the recognized escort of the Rightbody party, having been a former correspondent of her father's. He had been hired like any other guide, but had undertaken the task with that chivalrous enthusiasm which the average Californian always extends to the sex so rare to him. But the illusion had passed; and he had dropped into a sulky, practical sense of his situation, perhaps fraught with less danger to himself. Only when appealed to by his manhood or her weakness, he had forgotten his wounded vanity.

He strode moodily ahead, dutifully breaking the path for her in the direction of the distant canyon, where Mrs. Rightbody and her friend awaited them. Miss Alice was first to speak. In this trackless, uncharted terra incognita of the passions, it is always the woman who steps out to lead the way.

"You know this place very well. I suppose you have lived here long?"

"Yes."

"You were not born here--no?"

A long pause.

"I observe they call you 'Stanislaus Joe.' Of course that is not your real name?" (Mem.--Miss Alice had never called him ANYTHING, usually prefacing any request with a languid, "O-er-er, please, mister-er-a!" explicit enough for his station.)

"No."

Miss Alice (trotting after him, and bawling in his ear).--"WHAT name did you say?"

The Man (doggedly).--"I don't know." Nevertheless, when they reached the cabin, after an half-hour's buffeting with the storm, Miss Alice applied herself to her mother's escort, Mr. Ryder.

"What's the name of the man who takes care of my horse?"

"Stanislaus Joe," responded Mr. Ryder.

"Is that all?"

"No. Sometimes he's called Joe Stanislaus."

Miss Alice (satirically).--"I suppose it's the custom here to send young ladies out with gentlemen who hide their names under an alias?"

Mr. Ryder (greatly perplexed).--"Why, dear me, Miss Alice, you allers 'peared to me as a gal as was able to take keer--"

Miss Alice (interrupting with a wounded, dove-like timidity).--"Oh, never mind, please!"

The cabin offered but scanty accommodation to the tourists; which fact, when indignantly presented by Mrs. Rightbody, was explained by the good-humored Ryder from the circumstance that the usual hotel was only a slight affair of boards, cloth, and paper, put up during the season, and partly dismantled in the fall. "You couldn't be kept warm enough there," he added. Nevertheless Miss Alice noticed that both Mr. Ryder and Stanislaus Joe retired there with their pipes, after having prepared the ladies' supper, with the assistance of an Indian woman, who apparently emerged from the earth at the coming of the party, and disappeared as mysteriously.

The stars came out brightly before they slept; and the next morning a clear, unwinking sun beamed with almost summer power through the shutterless window of their cabin, and ironically disclosed the details of its rude interior. Two or three mangy, half-eaten buffalo-robes, a bearskin, some suspicious-looking blankets, rifles and saddles, deal-tables, and barrels, made up its scant inventory. A strip of faded calico hung before a recess near the chimney, but so blackened by smoke and age that even feminine curiosity respected its secret. Mrs. Rightbody was in high spirits, and informed her daughter that she was at last on the track of her husband's unknown correspondent. "Seventy-Four and Seventy-Five represent two members of the Vigilance Committee, my dear, and Mr. Ryder will assist me to find them."

"Mr. Ryder!" ejaculated Miss Alice, in scornful astonishment.

"Alice," said Mrs. Rightbody, with a suspicious assumption of sudden defence, "you injure yourself, you injure me, by this exclusive attitude. Mr. Ryder is a friend of your father's, an exceedingly well-informed gentleman. I have not, of course, imparted to him the extent of my suspicions. But he can help me to what I must and will know. You might treat him a little more civilly--or, at least, a little better than you do his servant, your guide. Mr. Ryder is a gentleman, and not a paid courier."

Miss Alice was suddenly attentive. When she spoke again, she asked, "Why do you not find out something about this Silsbie--who died--or was hung--or something of that kind?"

"Child!" said Mrs. Rightbody, "don't you see there was no Silsbie, or, if there was, he was simply the confidant of that--woman?"

A knock at the door, announcing the presence of Mr. Ryder and Stanislaus Joe with the horses, checked Mrs. Rightbody's speech. As the animals were being packed, Mrs. Rightbody for a moment withdrew in confidential conversation with Mr. Ryder, and, to the young lady's still greater annoyance, left her alone with Stanislaus Joe. Miss Alice was not in good temper, but she felt it necessary to say something.

"I hope the hotel offers better quarters for travellers than this in summer," she began.

"It does."

"Then this does not belong to it?"

"No, ma'am."

"Who lives here, then?"

"I do."

"I beg your pardon," stammered Miss Alice, "I thought you lived where we hired--where we met you--in--in--You must excuse me."

"I'm not a regular guide; but as times were hard, and I was out of grub, I took the job."

"Out of grub!" "job!" And SHE was the "job." What would Henry Marvin say? It would nearly kill him. She began herself to feel a little frightened, and walked towards the door.

"One moment, miss!"

The young girl hesitated. The man's tone was surly, and yet indicated a certain kind of half-pathetic grievance. HER curiosity got the better of her prudence, and she turned back.

"This morning," he began hastily, "when we were coming down the valley, you picked me up twice."

"I picked YOU up?" repeated the astonished Alice.

"Yes, CONTRADICTED me: that's what I mean,--once when you said those rocks were volcanic, once when you said the flower you picked was a poppy. I didn't let on at the time, for it wasn't my say; but all the while you were talking I might have laid for you--"

"I don't understand you," said Alice haughtily.

"I might have entrapped you before folks. But I only want you to know that I'M right, and here are the books to show it."

He drew aside the dingy calico curtain, revealed a small shelf of bulky books, took down two large volumes,--one of botany, one of geology,--nervously sought his text, and put them in Alice's outstretched hands.

"I had no intention--" she began, half-proudly, half-embarrassedly.

"Am I right, miss?" he interrupted.

"I presume you are, if you say so."

"That's all, ma'am. Thank you!"

Before the girl had time to reply, he was gone. When he again returned, it was with her horse, and Mrs. Rightbody and Ryder were awaiting her. But Miss Alice noticed that his own horse was missing.

"Are you not going with us?" she asked.

"No, ma'am."

"Oh, indeed!"

Miss Alice felt her speech was a feeble conventionalism; but it was all she could say. She, however, DID something. Hitherto it had been her habit to systematically reject his assistance in mounting to her seat. Now she awaited him. As he approached, she smiled, and put out her little foot. He instantly stooped; she placed it in his hand, rose with a spring, and for one supreme moment Stanislaus Joe held her unresistingly in his arms. The next moment she was in the saddle; but in that brief interval of sixty seconds she had uttered a volume in a single sentence,--

"I hope you will forgive me!"

He muttered a reply, and turned his face aside quickly as if to hide it.

Miss Alice cantered forward with a smile, but pulled her hat down over her eyes as she joined her mother. She was blushing.

PART III.

Mr. Ryder was as good as his word. A day or two later he entered Mrs. Rightbody's parlor at the Chrysopolis Hotel in Stockton, with the information that he had seen the mysterious senders of the despatch, and that they were now in the office of the hotel waiting her pleasure. Mr. Ryder further informed her that these gentlemen had only stipulated that they should not reveal their real names, and that they be introduced to her simply as the respective "Seventy-Four" and "Seventy-Five" who had signed the despatch sent to the late Mr. Rightbody.

Mrs. Rightbody at first demurred to this; but, on the assurance from Mr. Ryder that this was the only condition on which an interview would be granted, finally consented.

"You will find them square men, even if they are a little rough, ma'am. But, if you'd like me to be present, I'll stop; though I reckon, if ye'd calkilated on that, you'd have had me take care o' your business by proxy, and not come yourself three thousand miles to do it."

Mrs. Rightbody believed it better to see them alone.

"All right, ma'am. I'll hang round out here; and ef ye should happen to have a ticklin' in your throat, and a bad spell o' coughin', I'll drop in, careless like, to see if you don't want them drops. Sabe?"

And with an exceedingly arch wink, and a slight familiar tap on Mrs. Rightbody's shoulder, which might have caused the late Mr. Rightbody to burst his sepulchre, he withdrew.

A very timid, hesitating tap on the door was followed by the entrance of two men, both of whom, in general size, strength, and uncouthness, were ludicrously inconsistent with their diffident announcement. They proceeded in Indian file to the centre of the room, faced Mrs. Rightbody, acknowledged her deep courtesy by a strong shake of the hand, and, drawing two chairs opposite to her, sat down side by side.

"I presume I have the pleasure of addressing--" began Mrs. Rightbody.

The man directly opposite Mrs. Rightbody turned to the other inquiringly.

The other man nodded his head, and replied,--

"Seventy-Four."

"Seventy-Five," promptly followed the other.

Mrs. Rightbody paused, a little confused.

"I have sent for you," she began again, "to learn something more of the circumstances under which you gentlemen sent a despatch to my late husband."

"The circumstances," replied Seventy-Four quietly, with a side-glance at his companion, "panned out about in this yer style. We hung a man named Josh Silsbie, down at Deadwood, for hoss-stealin'. When I say WE, I speak for Seventy-Five yer as is present, as well as representin', so to speak, seventy-two other gents as is scattered. We hung Josh Silsbie on squar, pretty squar, evidence. Afore he was strung up, Seventy-Five yer axed him, accordin' to custom, ef ther was enny thing he had to say, or enny request that he allowed to make of us. He turns to Seventy-Five yer, and--"

Here he paused suddenly, looking at his companion.

"He sez, sez he," began Seventy-Five, taking up the narrative,--"he sez, 'Kin I write a letter?' sez he. Sez I, 'Not much, ole man: ye've got no time.' Sez he, 'Kin I send a despatch by telegraph?' I sez, 'Heave ahead.' He sez,--these is his dientikal words,--'Send to Adam Rightbody, Boston. Tell him to remember his sacred compack with me thirty years ago.'"

"'His sacred compack with me thirty years ago,'" echoed Seventy-Four,--"his dientikal words."

"What was the compact?" asked Mrs. Rightbody anxiously.

Seventy-Four looked at Seventy-Five, and then both arose, and retired to the corner of the parlor, where they engaged in a slow but whispered deliberation. Presently they returned, and sat down again.

"We allow," said Seventy-Four, quietly but decidedly, "that YOU know what that sacred compact was."

Mrs. Rightbody lost her temper and her truthfulness together. "Of course," she said hurriedly, "I know. But do you mean to say that you gave this poor man no further chance to explain before you murdered him?"

Seventy-Four and Seventy-Five both rose again slowly, and retired. When they returned again, and sat down, Seventy-Five, who by this time, through some subtle magnetism, Mrs. Rightbody began to recognize as the superior power, said gravely,--

"We wish to say, regarding this yer murder, that Seventy-Four and me is equally responsible; that we reckon also to represent, so to speak, seventy-two other gentlemen as is scattered; that we are ready, Seventy-Four and me, to take and holt that responsibility, now and at any time, afore every man or men as kin be fetched agin us. We wish to say that this yer say of ours holds good yer in Californy, or in any part of these United States."

"Or in Canady," suggested Seventy-Four.

"Or in Canady. We wouldn't agree to cross the water, or go to furrin parts, unless absolutely necessary. We leaves the chise of weppings to your principal, ma'am, or being a lady, ma'am, and interested, to any one you may fetch to act for him. An advertisement in any of the Sacramento papers, or a playcard or handbill stuck unto a tree near Deadwood, saying that Seventy-Four or Seventy-Five will communicate with this yer principal or agent of yours, will fetch us--allers."

Mrs. Rightbody, a little alarmed and desperate, saw her blunder. "I mean nothing of the kind," she said hastily. "I only expected that you might have some further details of this interview with Silsbie; that perhaps you could tell me--" a bold, bright thought crossed Mrs. Rightbody's mind--"something more about HER."

The two men looked at each other.

"I suppose your society have no objection to giving me information about HER," said Mrs. Rightbody eagerly.

Another quiet conversation in the corner, and the return of both men.

"We want to say that we've no objection."

Mrs. Rightbody's heart beat high. Her boldness had made her penetration good. Yet she felt she must not alarm the men heedlessly.

"Will you inform me to what extent Mr. Rightbody, my late husband, was interested in her?"

This time it seemed an age to Mrs. Rightbody before the men returned from their solemn consultation in the corner. She could both hear and feel that their discussion was more animated than their previous conferences. She was a little mortified, however, when they sat down, to hear Seventy-Four say slowly,--

"We wish to say that we don't allow to say HOW much."

"Do you not think that the 'sacred compact' between Mr. Rightbody and Mr. Silsbie referred to her?"

"We reckon it do."

Mrs. Rightbody, flushed and animated, would have given worlds had her daughter been present to hear this undoubted confirmation of her theory. Yet she felt a little nervous and uncomfortable even on this threshold of discovery.

"Is she here now?"

"She's in Tuolumne," said Seventy-Four.

"A little better looked arter than formerly," added Seventy-Five.

"I see. Then Mr. Silsbie ENTICED her away?"

"Well, ma'am, it WAS allowed as she runned away. But it wasn't proved, and it generally wasn't her style."

Mrs. Rightbody trifled with her next question.

"She was pretty, of course?"

The eyes of both men brightened.

"She was THAT!" said Seventy-Four emphatically.

"It would have done you good to see her!" added Seventy-Five.

Mrs. Rightbody inwardly doubted it; but, before she could ask another question, the two men again retired to the corner for consultation. When they came back, there was a shade more of kindliness and confidence in their manner; and Seventy-Four opened his mind more freely.

"We wish to say, ma'am, looking at the thing, by and large, in a far-minded way, that, ez YOU seem interested, and ez Mr. Rightbody was interested, and was, according to all accounts, deceived and led away by Silsbie, that we don't mind listening to any proposition YOU might make, as a lady--allowin' you was ekally interested."

"I understand," said Mrs. Rightbody quickly. "And you will furnish me with any papers?"

The two men again consulted.

"We wish to say, ma'am, that we think she's got papers, but--"

"I MUST have them, you understand," interrupted Mrs. Rightbody, "at any price.

"We was about to say, ma'am," said Seventy-Four slowly, "that, considerin' all things,--and you being a lady--you kin have HER, papers, pedigree, and guaranty, for twelve hundred dollars."

It has been alleged that Mrs. Rightbody asked only one question more, and then fainted. It is known, however, that by the next day it was understood in Deadwood that Mrs. Rightbody had confessed to the Vigilance Committee that her husband, a celebrated Boston millionaire, anxious to gain possession of Abner Springer's well-known sorrel mare, had incited the unfortunate Josh Silsbie to steal it; and that finally, failing in this, the widow of the deceased Boston millionaire was now in personal negotiation with the owners.

Howbeit, Miss Alice, returning home that afternoon, found her mother with a violent headache.

"We will leave here by the next steamer," said Mrs. Rightbody languidly. "Mr. Ryder has promised to accompany us."

"But, mother--"

"The climate, Alice, is over-rated. My nerves are already suffering from it. The associations are unfit for you, and Mr. Marvin is naturally impatient."

Miss Alice colored slightly.

"But your quest, mother?"

"I've abandoned it."

"But I have not," said Alice quietly. "Do you remember my guide at the Yo Semite,--Stanislaus Joe? Well, Stanislaus Joe is--who do you think?"

Mrs. Rightbody was languidly indifferent.

"Well, Stanislaus Joe is the son of Joshua Silsbie."

Mrs. Rightbody sat upright in astonishment

"Yes. But mother, he knows nothing of what we know. His father treated him shamefully, and set him cruelly adrift years ago; and, when he was hung, the poor fellow, in sheer disgrace, changed his name."

"But, if he knows nothing of his father's compact, of what interest is this?"

"Oh, nothing! Only I thought it might lead to something."

Mrs. Rightbody suspected that "something," and asked sharply, "And pray how did YOU find it out? You did not speak of it in the valley."

"Oh! I didn't find it out till to-day," said Miss Alice, walking to the window. "He happened to be here, and--told me."

PART IV.

If Mrs. Rightbody's friends had been astounded by her singular and unexpected pilgrimage to California so soon after her husband's decease, they were still more astounded by the information, a year later, that she was engaged to be married to a Mr. Ryder, of whom only the scant history was known, that he was a Californian, and former correspondent of her husband. It was undeniable that the man was wealthy, and evidently no mere adventurer; it was rumored that he was courageous and manly: but even those who delighted in his odd humor were shocked at his grammar and slang.

It was said that Mr. Marvin had but one interview with his father-in-law elect, and returned so supremely disgusted, that the match was broken off. The horse-stealing story, more or less garbled, found its way through lips that pretended to decry it, yet eagerly repeated it. Only one member of the Rightbody family--and a new one--saved them from utter ostracism. It was young Mr. Ryder, the adopted son of the prospective head of the household, whose culture, manners, and general elegance, fascinated and thrilled Boston with a new sensation. It seemed to many that Miss Alice should, in the vicinity of this rare exotic, forget her former enthusiasm for a professional life; but the young man was pitied by society, and various plans for diverting him from any mesalliance with the Rightbody family were concocted.

It was a wintry night, and the second anniversary of Mr. Rightbody's death, that a light was burning in his library. But the dead man's chair was occupied by young Mr. Ryder, adopted son of the new proprietor of the mansion; and before him stood Alice, with her dark eyes fixed on the table.

"There must have been something in it, Joe, believe me. Did you never hear your father speak of mine?"

"Never."

"But you say he was college-bred, and born a gentleman, and in his youth he must have had many friends."

"Alice," said the young man gravely, "when I have done something to redeem my name, and wear it again before these people, before YOU, it would be well to revive the past. But till then--"

But Alice was not to be put down. "I remember," she went on, scarcely heeding him, "that, when I came in that night, papa was reading a letter, and seemed to be disconcerted."

"A letter?"

"Yes; but," added Alice, with a sigh, "when we found him here insensible, there was no letter on his person. He must have destroyed it."

"Did you ever look among his papers? If found, it might be a clew."

The young man glanced toward the cabinet. Alice read his eyes, and answered,--

"Oh, dear, no! The cabinet contained only his papers, all perfectly arranged,--you know how methodical were his habits,--and some old business and private letters, all carefully put away."

"Let us see them," said the young man, rising.

They opened drawer after drawer; files upon files of letters and business papers, accurately folded and filed. Suddenly Alice uttered a little cry, and picked up a quaint ivory paper-knife lying at the bottom of a drawer.

"It was missing the next day, and never could be found: he must have mislaid it here. This is the drawer," said Alice eagerly.

Here was a clew. But the lower part of the drawer was filled with old letters, not labelled, yet neatly arranged in files. Suddenly he stopped, and said, "Put them back, Alice, at once."

"Why?"

"Some of these letters are in my father's handwriting."

"The more reason why I should see them," said the girl imperatively. "Here, you take part, and I'll take part, and we'll get through quicker."

There was a certain decision and independence in her manner which he had learned to respect. He took the letters, and in silence read them with her. They were old college letters, so filled with boyish dreams, ambitions, aspirations, and utopian theories, that I fear neither of these young people even recognized their parents in the dead ashes of the past. They were both grave, until Alice uttered a little hysterical cry, and dropped her face in her hands. Joe was instantly beside her.

"It's nothing, Joe, nothing. Don't read it, please; please, don't. It's so funny! it's so very queer!"

But Joe had, after a slight, half-playful struggle, taken the letter from the girl. Then he read aloud the words written by his father thirty years ago.

"I thank you, dear friend, for all you say about my wife and boy. I thank you for reminding me of our boyish compact. He will be ready to fulfil it, I know, if he loves those his father loves, even if you should marry years later. I am glad for your sake, for both our sakes, that it is a boy. Heaven send you a good wife, dear Adams, and a daughter, to make my son equally happy."

Joe Silsbie looked down, took the half-laughing, half-tearful face in his hands, kissed her forehead, and, with tears in his grave eyes, said, "Amen!"

*****

I am inclined to think that this sentiment was echoed heartily by Mrs. Rightbody's former acquaintances, when, a year later, Miss Alice was united to a professional gentleman of honor and renown, yet who was known to be the son of a convicted horse-thief. A few remembered the previous Californian story, and found corroboration therefor; but a majority believed it a just reward to Miss Alice for her conduct to Mr. Marvin, and, as Miss Alice cheerfully accepted it in that light, I do not see why I may not end my story with happiness to all concerned.

A LEGEND OF SAMMTSTADT.

It was the sacred hour of noon at Sammtstadt. Everybody was at dinner; and the serious Kellner of "Der Wildemann" glanced in mild reproach at Mr. James Clinch, who, disregarding that fact and the invitatory table d'hote, stepped into the street. For Mr. Clinch had eaten a late breakfast at Gladbach, was dyspeptic and American, and, moveover, preoccupied with business. He was consequently indignant, on entering the garden-like court and cloister-like counting-house of "Von Becheret, Sons, Uncles, and Cousins," to find the comptoir deserted even by the porter, and was furious at the maidservant, who offered the sacred shibboleth "Mittagsessen" as a reasonable explanation of the solitude. "A country," said Mr. Clinch to himself, "that stops business at mid-day to go to dinner, and employs women-servants to talk to business-men, is played out."

He stepped from the silent building into the equally silent Kronprinzen Strasse. Not a soul to be seen anywhere. Rows on rows of two-storied, gray-stuccoed buildings that might be dwellings, or might be offices, all showing some traces of feminine taste and supervision in a flower or a curtain that belied the legended "Comptoir," or "Direction," over their portals. Mr. Clinch thought of Boston and State Street, of New York and Wall Street, and became coldly contemptuous.

Yet there was clearly nothing to do but to walk down the formal rows of chestnuts that lined the broad Strasse, and then walk back again. At the corner of the first cross-street he was struck with the fact that two men who were standing in front of a dwelling-house appeared to be as inconsistent, and out of proportion to the silent houses, as were the actors on a stage to the painted canvas thoroughfares before which they strutted. Mr. Clinch usually had no fancies, had no eye for quaintness; besides, this was not a quaint nor romantic district, only an entrepot for silks and velvets, and Mr. Clinch was here, not as a tourist, but as a purchaser. The guidebooks had ignored Sammtstadt, and he was too good an American to waste time in looking up uncatalogued curiosities. Besides, he had been here once before,--an entire day!

One o'clock. Still a full hour and a half before his friend would return to business. What should he do? The Verein where he had once been entertained was deserted even by its waiters; the garden, with its ostentatious out-of-door tables, looked bleak and bare. Mr. Clinch was not artistic in his tastes; but even he was quick to detect the affront put upon Nature by this continental, theatrical gardening, and turned disgustedly away. Born near a "lake" larger than the German Ocean, he resented a pool of water twenty-five feet in diameter under that alluring title; and, a frequenter of the Adirondacks, he could scarce contain himself over a bit of rock-work twelve feet high. "A country," said Mr. Clinch, "that--" but here he remembered that he had once seen in a park in his native city an imitation of the Drachenfels in plaster, on a scale of two inches to the foot, and checked his speech.

He turned into the principal allee of the town. There was a long white building at one end,--the Bahnhof: at the other end he remembered a dye-house. He had, a year ago, met its hospitable proprietor: he would call upon him now.

But the same solitude confronted him as he passed the porter's lodge beside the gateway. The counting-house, half villa, half factory, must have convoked its humanity in some out-of-the-way refectory, for the halls and passages were tenantless. For the first time he began to be impressed with a certain foreign quaintness in the surroundings; he found himself also recalling something he had read when a boy, about an enchanted palace whose inhabitants awoke on the arrival of a long-predestined Prince. To assure himself of the absolute ridiculousness of this fancy, he took from his pocket the business-card of its proprietor, a sample of dye, and recalled his own personality in a letter of credit. Having dismissed this idea from his mind, he lounged on again through a rustic lane that might have led to a farmhouse, yet was still, absurdly enough, a part of the factory gardens. Crossing a ditch by a causeway, he presently came to another ditch and another causeway, and then found himself idly contemplating a massive, ivy-clad, venerable brick wall. As a mere wall it might not have attracted his attention; but it seemed to enter and bury itself at right angles in the side-wall of a quite modern-looking dwelling. After satisfying himself of this fact, he passed on before the dwelling, but was amazed to see the wall reappear on the other side exactly the same--old, ivy-grown, sturdy, uncompromising, and ridiculous.

Could it actually be a part of the house? He turned back, and repassed the front of the building. The entrance door was hospitably open. There was a hall and a staircase, but--by all that was preposterous!--they were built OVER and AROUND the central brick intrusion. The wall actually ran through the house! "A country," said Mr. Clinch to himself, "where they build their houses over ruins to accommodate them, or save the trouble of removal, is,--" but a very pleasant voice addressing him here stopped his usual hasty conclusion.

"Guten Morgen!"

Mr. Clinch looked hastily up. Leaning on the parapet of what appeared to be a garden on the roof of the house was a young girl, red-cheeked, bright-eyed, blond-haired. The voice was soft, subdued, and mellow; it was part of the new impression he was receiving, that it seemed to be in some sort connected with the ivy-clad wall before him. His hat was in his hand as he answered,--

"Guten Morgen!"

"Was the Herr seeking anything?"

"The Herr was only waiting a longtime-coming friend, and had strayed here to speak with the before-known proprietor."

"So? But, the before-known proprietor sleeping well at present after dinner, would the Herr on the terrace still a while linger?"

The Herr would, but looked around in vain for the means to do it. He was thinking of a scaling-ladder, when the young woman reappeared at the open door, and bade him enter.

Following the youthful hostess, Mr. Clinch mounted the staircase, but, passing the mysterious wall, could not forbear an allusion to it. "It is old, very old," said the girl: "it was here when I came."

"That was not very long ago," said Mr. Clinch gallantly.

"No; but my grandfather found it here too."

"And built over it?"

"Why not? It is very, very hard, and SO thick."

Mr. Clinch here explained, with masculine superiority, the existence of such modern agents as nitro-glycerine and dynamite, persuasive in their effects upon time-honored obstructions and encumbrances.

"But there was not then what you call--this--ni--nitro-glycerine."

"But since then?"

The young girl gazed at him in troubled surprise. "My great-grandfather did not take it away when he built the house: why should we?"

"Oh!"

They had passed through a hall and dining-room, and suddenly stepped out of a window upon a gravelled terrace. From this a few stone steps descended to another terrace, on which trees and shrubs were growing; and yet, looking over the parapet, Mr. Clinch could see the road some twenty feet below. It was nearly on a level with, and part of, the second story of the house. Had an earthquake lifted the adjacent ground? or had the house burrowed into a hill? Mr. Clinch turned to his companion, who was standing close beside him, breathing quite audibly, and leaving an impression on his senses as of a gentle and fragrant heifer.

"How was all this done?"

The maiden did not know. "It was always here."

Mr. Clinch reascended the steps. He had quite forgotten his impatience. Possibly it was the gentle, equable calm of the girl, who, but for her ready color, did not seem to be moved by anything; perhaps it was the peaceful repose of this mausoleum of the dead and forgotten wall that subdued him, but he was quite willing to take the old-fashioned chair on the terrace which she offered him, and follow her motions with not altogether mechanical eyes as she drew out certain bottles and glasses from a mysterious closet in the wall. Mr. Clinch had the weakness of a majority of his sex in believing that he was a good judge of wine and women. The latter, as shown in the specimen before him, he would have invoiced as a fair sample of the middle-class German woman,--healthy, comfort-loving, home-abiding, the very genius of domesticity. Even in her virgin outlines the future wholesome matron was already forecast, from the curves of her broad hips, to the flat lines of her back and shoulders. Of the wine he was to judge later. THAT required an even more subtle and unimpassioned intellect.

She placed two bottles before him on the table,--one, the traditional long-necked, amber-colored Rheinflasche; the other, an old, quaint, discolored, amphorax-patterned glass jug. The first she opened.

"This," she said, pointing to the other, "cannot be opened."

Mr. Clinch paid his respects first to the opened bottle, a good quality of Niersteiner. With his intellect thus clarified, he glanced at the other.

"It is from my great-grandfather. It is old as the wall."

Mr. Clinch examined the bottle attentively. It seemed to have no cork. Formed of some obsolete, opaque glass, its twisted neck was apparently hermetically sealed by the same material. The maiden smiled, as she said,--

"It cannot be opened now without breaking the bottle. It is not good luck to do so. My grandfather and my father would not."

But Mr. Clinch was still examining the bottle. Its neck was flattened towards the mouth; but a close inspection showed it was closed by some equally hard cement, but not glass.

"If I can open it without breaking the bottle, have I your permission?"

A mischievous glance rested on Mr. Clinch, as the maiden answered,--

"I shall not object; but for what will you do it?"

"To taste it, to try it."

"You are not afraid?"

There was just enough obvious admiration of Mr. Clinch's audacity in the maiden's manner to impel him to any risk. His only answer was to take from his pocket a small steel instrument. Holding the neck of the bottle firmly in one hand, he passed his thumb and the steel twice or thrice around it. A faint rasping, scratching sound was all the wondering girl heard. Then, with a sudden, dexterous twist of his thumb and finger, to her utter astonishment he laid the top of the neck, neatly cut off, in her hand.

"There's a better and more modern bottle than you had before," he said, pointing to the cleanly-divided neck, "and any cork will fit it now."

But the girl regarded him with anxiety. "And you still wish to taste the wine?"

"With your permission, yes!"

He looked up in her eyes. There was permission: there was something more, that was flattering to his vanity. He took the wine-glass, and, slowly and in silence, filled it from the mysterious flask.

The wine fell into the glass clearly, transparently, heavily, but still and cold as death. There was no sparkle, no cheap ebullition, no evanescent bubble. Yet it was so clear, that, but for a faint amber-tinting, the glass seemed empty. There was no aroma, no ethereal diffusion from its equable surface. Perhaps it was fancy, perhaps it was from nervous excitement; but a slight chill seemed to radiate from the still goblet, and bring down the temperature of the terrace. Mr. Clinch and his companion both insensibly shivered.

But only for a moment. Mr. Clinch raised the glass to his lips. As he did so, he remembered seeing distinctly, as in a picture before him, the sunlit terrace, the pretty girl in the foreground,--an amused spectator of his sacrilegious act,--the outlying ivy-crowned wall, the grass-grown ditch, the tall factory chimneys rising above the chestnuts, and the distant poplars that marked the Rhine.

The wine was delicious; perhaps a TRIFLE, only a trifle, heady. He was conscious of a slight exaltation. There was also a smile upon the girl's lip and a roguish twinkle in her eye as she looked at him.

"Do you find the wine to your taste?" she asked.

"Fair enough, I warrant," said Mr. Clinch with ponderous gallantry; "but methinks 'tis nothing compared with the nectar that grows on those ruby lips. Nay, by St. Ursula, I swear it!"

No sooner had this solemnly ridiculous speech passed the lips of the unfortunate man than he would have given worlds to have recalled it. He knew that he must be intoxicated; that the sentiment and language were utterly unlike him, he was miserably aware; that he did not even know exactly what it meant, he was also hopelessly conscious. Yet feeling all this,--feeling, too, the shame of appearing before her as a man who had lost his senses through a single glass of wine,--nevertheless he rose awkwardly, seized her hand, and by sheer force drew her towards him, and kissed her. With an exclamation that was half a cry and half a laugh, she fled from him, leaving him alone and bewildered on the terrace.

For a moment Mr. Clinch supported himself against the open window, leaning his throbbing head on the cold glass. Shame, mortification, an hysterical half-consciousness of his utter ridiculousness, and yet an odd, undefined terror of something, by turns possessed him. Was he ever before guilty of such perfect folly? Had he ever before made such a spectacle of himself? Was it possible that he, Mr. James Clinch, the coolest head at a late supper,--he, the American, who had repeatedly drunk Frenchmen and Englishmen under the table--could be transformed into a sentimental, stagey idiot by a single glass of wine? He was conscious, too, of asking

himself these very questions in a stilted sort of rhetoric, and with a rising brutality of anger that was new to him. And then everything swam before him, and he
seemed to lose all consciousness.

But only for an instant. With a strong effort of his will he again recalled himself, his situation, his surroundings, and, above all, his appointment. He rose to his
feet, hurriedly descended the terrace-steps, and, before he well knew how, found
himself again on the road. Once there, his faculties returned in full vigor; he was
again himself. He strode briskly forward toward the ditch he had crossed only a few
moments before, but was suddenly stopped. It was filled with water. He looked up
and down. It was clearly the same ditch; but a flowing stream thirty feet wide now
separated him from the other bank.

The appearance of this unlooked-for obstacle made Mr. Clinch doubt the full
restoration of his faculties. He stepped to the brink of the flood to bathe his head in
the stream, and wash away the last vestiges of his potations. But as he approached
the placid depths, and knelt down he again started back, and this time with a full
conviction of his own madness; for reflected from its mirror-like surface was a figure he could scarcely call his own, although here and there some trace of his former
self remained.

His close-cropped hair, trimmed a la mode, had given way to long, curling locks
that dropped upon his shoulders. His neat mustache was frightfully prolonged, and
curled up at the ends stiffly. His Piccadilly collar had changed shape and texture,
and reached--a mass of lace--to a point midway of his breast! His boots,--why had
he not noticed his boots before?--these triumphs of his Parisian bootmaker, were
lost in hideous leathern cases that reached half way up his thighs. In place of his
former high silk hat, there lay upon the ground beside him the awful thing he had
just taken off,--a mass of thickened felt, flap, feather, and buckle that weighed at
least a stone.

A single terrible idea now took possession of him. He had been "sold," "taken
in," "done for." He saw it all. In a state of intoxication he had lost his way, had been
dragged into some vile den, stripped of his clothes and valuables, and turned adrift
upon the quiet town in this shameless masquerade. How should he keep his appointment? how inform the police of this outrage upon a stranger and an American
citizen? how establish his identity? Had they spared his papers? He felt feverishly

in his breast. Ah!--his watch? Yes, a watch--heavy, jewelled, enamelled--and, by all that was ridiculous, FIVE OTHERS! He ran his hands into his capacious trunk hose. What was this? Brooches, chains, finger-rings,--one large episcopal one,--ear-rings, and a handful of battered gold and silver coins. His papers, his memorandums, his passport--all proofs of his identity--were gone! In their place was the unmistakable omnium gatherum of an accomplished knight of the road. Not only was his personality, but his character, gone forever.

It was a part of Mr. Clinch's singular experience that this last stroke of ill fortune seemed to revive in him something of the brutal instinct he had felt a moment before. He turned eagerly about with the intention of calling some one--the first person he met--to account. But the house that he had just quitted was gone. The wall! Ah, there it was, no longer purposeless, intrusive, and ivy-clad, but part of the buttress of another massive wall that rose into battlements above him. Mr. Clinch turned again hopelessly toward Sammtstadt. There was the fringe of poplars on the Rhine, there were the outlying fields lit by the same meridian sun; but the characteristic chimneys of Sammtstadt were gone. Mr. Clinch was hopelessly lost.

The sound of a horn breaking the stillness recalled his senses. He now for the first time perceived that a little distance below him, partly hidden in the trees, was a queer, tower-shaped structure with chains and pulleys, that in some strange way recalled his boyish reading. A drawbridge and portcullis! And on the battlement a figure in a masquerading dress as absurd as his own, flourishing a banner and trumpet, and trying to attract his attention.

"Was wollen Sie?"

"I want to see the proprietor," said Mr. Clinch, choking back his rage.

There was a pause, and the figure turned apparently to consult with some one behind the battlements. After a moment he reappeared, and in a perfunctory monotone, with an occasional breathing spell on the trumpet, began,--

"You do give warranty as a good knight and true, as well as by the bones of the blessed St. Ursula, that you bear no ill will, secret enmity, wicked misprise or conspiracy, against the body of our noble lord and master Von Kolnsche? And you bring with you no ambush, siege, or surprise of retainers, neither secret warrant nor lettres de cachet, nor carry on your knightly person poisoned dagger, magic ring, witch-powder, nor enchanted bullet, and that you have entered into no unhallowed alliance with the Prince of Darkness, gnomes, hexies, dragons, Undines, Loreleis, nor the like?"

"Come down out of that, you d----d old fool!" roared Mr. Clinch, now perfectly beside himself with rage,--"come down, and let me in!"

As Mr. Clinch shouted out the last words, confused cries of recognition and welcome, not unmixed with some consternation, rose from the battlements: "Ach Gott!" "Mutter Gott--it is he! It is Jann, Der Wanderer. It is himself." The chains rattled, the ponderous drawbridge creaked and dropped; and across it a medley of motley figures rushed pellmell. But, foremost among them, the very maiden whom he had left not ten minutes before flew into his arms, and with a cry of joyful greeting sank upon his breast. Mr. Clinch looked down upon the fair head and long braids. It certainly was the same maiden, his cruel enchantress; but where did she get those absurd garments?

"Willkommen," said a stout figure, advancing with some authority, and seizing his disengaged hand, "where hast thou been so long?"

Mr. Clinch, by no means placated, coldly dropped the extended hand. It was NOT the proprietor he had known. But there was a singular resemblance in his face to some one of Mr. Clinch's own kin; but who, he could not remember. "May I take the liberty of asking your name?" he asked coldly.

The figure grinned. "Surely; but, if thou standest upon punctilio, it is for ME to ask thine, most noble Freiherr," said he, winking upon his retainers. "Whom have I the honor of entertaining?"

"My name is Clinch,--James Clinch of Chicago, Ill."

A shout of laughter followed. In the midst of his rage and mortification Mr. Clinch fancied he saw a shade of pain and annoyance flit across the face of the maiden. He was puzzled, but pressed her hand, in spite of his late experiences, reassuringly. She made a gesture of silence to him, and then slipped away in the crowd.

"Schames K'l'n'sche von Schekargo," mimicked the figure, to the unspeakable delight of his retainers. "So! THAT is the latest French style. Holy St. Ursula! Hark ye, nephew! I am not a travelled man. Since the Crusades we simple Rhine gentlemen have staid at home. But I call myself Kolnsche of Koln, at your service."

"Very likely you are right," said Mr. Clinch hotly, disregarding the caution of his fair companion; "but, whoever YOU are, I am a stranger entitled to protection.

I have been robbed."

If Mr. Clinch had uttered an exquisite joke instead of a very angry statement, it could not have been more hilariously received. He paused, grew confused, and then went on hesitatingly,--

"In place of my papers and credentials I find only these." And he produced the jewelry from his pockets.

Another shout of laughter and clapping of hands followed this second speech; and the baron, with a wink at his retainers, prolonged the general mirth by saying, "By the way, nephew, there is little doubt but there has been robbery--somewhere."

"It was done," continued Mr. Clinch, hurrying to make an end of his explanation, "while I was inadvertently overcome with liquor,--drugged liquor."

The laughter here was so uproarious that the baron, albeit with tears of laughter in his own eyes, made a peremptory gesture of silence. The gesture was peculiar to the baron, efficacious and simple. It consisted merely in knocking down the nearest laugher. Having thus restored tranquillity, he strode forward, and took Mr. Clinch by the hand. "By St. Adolph, I did doubt thee a moment ago, nephew; but this last frank confession of thine shows me I did thee wrong. Willkommen zu Hause, Jann, drunk or sober, willcommen zu Cracowen."

More and more mystified, but convinced of the folly of any further explanation, Mr. Clinch took the extended hand of his alleged uncle, and permitted himself to be led into the castle. They passed into a large banqueting-hall adorned with armor and implements of the chase. Mr. Clinch could not help noticing, that, although the appointments were liberal and picturesque, the ventilation was bad, and the smoke from the huge chimney made the air murky. The oaken tables, massive in carving and rich in color, were unmistakably greasy; and Mr. Clinch slipped on a piece of meat that one of the dozen half-wild dogs who were occupying the room was tearing on the floor. The dog, yelping, ran between the legs of a retainer, precipitating him upon the baron, who instantly, with the "equal foot" of fate, kicked him and the dog into a corner.

"And whence came you last?" asked the baron, disregarding the little contretemps, and throwing himself heavily on an oaken settle, while he pushed a queer, uncomfortable-looking stool, with legs like a Siamese-twin-connected double X, towards his companion.

Mr. Clinch, who had quite given himself up to fate, answered mechanically,-- "Paris."

The baron winked his eye with unutterable, elderly wickedness. "Ach Gott! it is nothing to what it was when I was your age. Ah! there was Manon,--Sieur Manon we used to call her. I suppose she's getting old now. How goes on the feud between the students and the citizens? Eh? Did you go to the bal in la Cite?"

Mr. Clinch stopped the flow of those Justice-Shallow-like reminiscences by an uneasy exclamation. He was thinking of the maiden who had disappeared so suddenly. The baron misinterpreted his nervousness. "What ho, within there!--Max, Wolfgang,--lazy rascals! Bring some wine."

At the baleful word Mr. Clinch started to his feet. "Not for me! Bring me none of your body-and-soul-destroying poison! I've enough of it!"

The baron stared. The servitors stared also.

"I beg your pardon," said Mr. Clinch, recalling himself slowly; "but I fear that Rhine wine does not agree with me."

The baron grinned. Perceiving, however, that the three servitors grinned also, he kicked two of them into obscurity, and felled the third to the floor with his fist. "Hark ye, nephew," he said, turning to the astonished Clinch, "give over this nonsense! By the mitre of Bishop Hatto, thou art as big a fool as he!"

"Hatto," repeated Clinch mechanically. "What! he of the Mouse Tower?"

"Ay, of the Mouse Tower!" sneered the baron. "I see you know the story."

"Why am I like him?" asked Mr. Clinch in amazement.

The baron grinned. "HE punished the Rhenish wine as thou dost, without judgment. He had--"

"The jim-jams," said Mr. Clinch mechanically again.

The baron frowned. "I know not what gibberish thou sayest by 'jim-jams'; but he had, like thee, the wildest fantasies and imaginings; saw snakes, toads, rats, in his boots, but principally rats; said they pursued him, came to his room, his bed--ach Gott!"

"Oh!" said Mr. Clinch, with a sudden return to his firmer self and his native inquiring habits; "then THAT is the fact about Bishop Hatto of the story?"

"His enemies made it the subject of a vile slander of an old friend of mine," said the baron; "and those cursed poets, who believe everything, and then persuade others to do so,--may the Devil fly away with them!--kept it up."

Here were facts quite to Mr. Clinch's sceptical mind. He forgot himself and his surroundings.

"And that story of the Drachenfels?" he asked insinuatingly,--"the dragon, you know. Was he too--"

The baron grinned. "A boar transformed by the drunken brains of the Bauers of the Siebengebirge. Ach Gott! Ottefried had many a hearty laugh over it; and it did him, as thou knowest, good service with the nervous mother of the silly maiden."

"And the seven sisters of Schonberg?" asked Mr. Clinch persuasively.

"'Schonberg! Seven sisters!' What of them?" demanded the baron sharply.

"Why, you know,--the maidens who were so coy to their suitors, and--don't you remember?--jumped into the Rhine to avoid them."

"'Coy? Jumped into the Rhine to avoid suitors'?" roared the baron, purple with rage. "Hark ye, nephew! I like not this jesting. Thou knowest I married one of the Schonberg girls, as did thy father. How 'coy' they were is neither here nor there; but mayhap WE might tell another story. Thy father, as weak a fellow as thou art where a petticoat is concerned, could not as a gentleman do other than he did. And THIS is his reward? Ach Gott! 'Coy!' And THIS, I warrant, is the way the story is delivered in Paris."

Mr. Clinch would have answered that this was the way he read it in a guide-book, but checked himself at the hopelessness of the explanation. Besides, he was on the eve of historic information; he was, as it were, interviewing the past; and, whether he would ever be able to profit by the opportunity or not, he could not bear to lose it. "And how about the Lorelei--is she, too, a fiction?" he asked glibly.

"It was said," observed the baron sardonically, "that when thou disappeared with the gamekeeper's daughter at Obercassel--Heaven knows where!--thou wast swallowed up in a whirlpool with some creature. Ach Gott! I believe it! But a truce to this balderdash. And so thou wantest to know of the 'coy' sisters of Schoenberg? Hark ye, Jann, that cousin of thine is a Schonberg. Call you her 'coy'? Did I not see thy greeting? Eh? By St. Adolph, knowing thee as she does to be robber and thief, call you her greeting 'coy'?"

Furious as Mr. Clinch inwardly became under these epithets, he felt that his explanation would hardly relieve the maiden from deceit, or himself from weakness. But out of his very perplexity and turmoil a bright idea was born. He turned to the baron,--

"Then you have no faith in the Rhine legends?"

The baron only replied with a contemptuous shrug of his shoulders.

"But what if I told you a new one?"

"You?"

"Yes; a part of my experience?"

The baron was curious. It was early in the afternoon, just after dinner. He might be worse bored.

"I've only one condition," added Mr. Clinch: "the young lady--I mean, of course, my cousin--must hear it too."

"Oh, ay! I see. Of course--the old trick! Well, call the jade. But mark ye, Sir Nephew, no enchanted maidens and knights. Keep to thyself. Be as thou art, vagabond Jann Kolnische, knight of the road.--What ho there, scoundrels! Call the Lady Wilhemina."

It was the first time Mr. Clinch had heard his fair friend's name; but it was not, evidently, the first time she had seen him, as the very decided wink the gentle maiden dropped him testified. Nevertheless, with hands lightly clasped together, and downcast eyes, she stood before them.

Mr. Clinch began. Without heeding the baron's scornful grin, he graphically described his meeting, two years before, with a Lorelei, her usual pressing invitation, and his subsequent plunge into the Rhine.

"I am free to confess," added Mr. Clinch, with an affecting glance to Wilhemina, "that I was not enamoured of the graces of the lady, but was actuated by my desire to travel, and explore hitherto unknown regions. I wished to travel, to visit--"

"Paris," interrupted the baron sarcastically.

"America," continued Mr. Clinch.

"What?"--"America."

"'Tis a gnome-like sounding name, this Meriker. Go on, nephew: tell us of Meriker."

With the characteristic fluency of his nation, Mr. Clinch described his landing on those enchanted shores, viz, the Rhine Whirlpool and Hell Gate, East River,

New York. He described the railways, tram-ways, telegraphs, hotels, phonograph, and telephone. An occasional oath broke from the baron, but he listened attentively; and in a few moments Mr. Clinch had the raconteur's satisfaction of seeing the vast hall slowly filling with open-eyed and open-mouthed retainers hanging upon his words. Mr. Clinch went on to describe his astonishment at meeting on these very shores some of his own blood and kin. "In fact," said Mr. Clinch, "here were a race calling themselves 'Clinch,' but all claiming to have descended from Kolnische."

"And how?" sneered the baron.

"Through James Kolnische and Wilhelmina his wife," returned Mr. Clinch boldly. "They emigrated from Koln and Crefeld to Philadelphia, where there is a quarter named Crefeld." Mr. Clinch felt himself shaky as to his chronology, but wisely remembered that it was a chronology of the future to his hearers, and they could not detect an anachronism. With his eyes fixed upon those of the gentle Wilhelmina, Mr. Clinch now proceeded to describe his return to his fatherland, but his astonishment at finding the very face of the country changed, and a city standing on those fields he had played in as a boy; and how he had wandered hopelessly on, until he at last sat wearily down in a humble cottage built upon the ruins of a lordly castle. "So utterly travel-worn and weak had I become," said Mr. Clinch, with adroitly simulated pathos, "that a single glass of wine offered me by the simple cottage maiden affected me like a prolonged debauch."

A long-drawn snore was all that followed this affecting climax. The baron was asleep; the retainers were also asleep. Only one pair of eyes remained open,--arch, luminous, blue,--Wilhelmina's.

"There is a subterranean passage below us to Linn. Let us fly!" she whispered.

"But why?"

"They always do it in the legends," she murmured modestly.

"But your father?"

"He sleeps. Do you not hear him?"

Certainly somebody was snoring. But, oddly enough, it seemed to be Wilhelmina. Mr. Clinch suggested this to her.

"Fool, it is yourself!"

Mr. Clinch, struck with the idea, stopped to consider. She was right. It certainly WAS himself.

With a struggle he awoke. The sun was shining. The maiden was looking at him. But the castle--the castle was gone!

"You have slept well," said the maiden archly. "Everybody does after dinner at Sammtstadt. Father has just awakened, and is coming."

Mr. Clinch stared at the maiden, at the terrace, at the sky, at the distant chimneys of Sammtstadt, at the more distant Rhine, at the table before him, and finally at the empty glass. The maiden smiled. "Tell me," said Mr. Clinch, looking in her eyes, "is there a secret passage underground between this place and the Castle of Linn?"

"An underground passage?"

"Ay--whence the daughter of the house fled with a stranger knight."

"They say there is," said the maiden, with a gentle blush.

"Can you show it to me?"

She hesitated. "Papa is coming: I'll ask him."

I presume she did. At least the Herr Consul at Sammtstadt informs me of a marriage-certificate issued to one Clinch of Chicago, and Kolnische of Koln; and there is an amusing story extant in the Verein at Sammtstadt, of an American connoisseur of Rhine wines, who mistook a flask of Cognac and rock-candy, used for "craftily qualifying" lower grades of wine to the American standard, for the rarest Rudesheimerberg.

VIEWS FROM A GERMAN SPION

Outside of my window, two narrow perpendicular mirrors, parallel with the casement, project into the street, yet with a certain unobtrusiveness of angle that enables them to reflect the people who pass, without any reciprocal disclosure of their own. The men and women hurrying by not only do not know they are observed, but, what is worse, do not even see their own reflection in this hypocritical plane, and are consequently unable, through its aid, to correct any carelessness of garb, gait, or demeanor. At first this seems to be taking an unfair advantage of the human animal, who invariably assumes an attitude when he is conscious of being under human focus. But I observe that my neighbors' windows, right and left, have a similar apparatus, that this custom is evidently a local one, and the locality is German. Being an American stranger, I am quite willing to leave the morality of the transaction with the locality, and adapt myself to the custom: indeed, I had thought of offering it, figuratively, as an excuse for any unfairness of observation I might make in these pages. But my German mirrors reflect without prejudice, selection, or comment; and the American eye, I fear, is but mortal, and like all mortal eyes, figuratively as well as in that literal fact noted by an eminent scientific authority, infinitely inferior to the work of the best German opticians.

And this leads me to my first observation, namely, that a majority of those who pass my mirror have weak eyes, and have already invoked the aid of the optician. Why are these people, physically in all else so much stronger than my countrymen, deficient in eyesight? Or, to omit the passing testimony of my Spion, and take my own personal experience, why does my young friend Max, brightest of all school-boys, who already wears the cap that denotes the highest class,--why does he shock me by suddenly drawing forth a pair of spectacles, that upon his fresh, rosy face would be an obvious mocking imitation of the Herr Papa--if German children could ever, by any possibility, be irreverent? Or why does the Fraulein Marie, his sister, pink as Aurora, round as Hebe, suddenly veil her blue eyes with a golden lorgnette in the midst of our polyglot conversation? Is it to evade the direct, admiring glance of the impulsive American? Dare I say NO? Dare I say that that frank, clear, honest, earnest return of the eye, which has on the Continent most unfairly brought my fair countrywomen under criticism, is quite as common to her more carefully-guarded, tradition-hedged German sisters? No, it is not that. Is it any thing in these emerald and opal tinted skies, which seem so unreal to the American eye, and for the first time explain what seemed the unreality of German art? in these mysterious yet restful Rhine fogs, which prolong the twilight, and hang the curtain of romance even over mid-day? Surely not. Is it not rather, O Herr Professor profound in analogy and philosophy!--is it not rather this abominable black-letter, this elsewhere-discarded, uncouth, slowly-decaying text known as the German Alphabet, that plucks out the bright eyes of youth, and bristles the gateways of your language with a chevaux de frise of splintered rubbish? Why must I hesitate whether it is an accident of the printer's press, or the poor quality of the paper, that makes this letter a "k" or a "t"? Why must I halt in an emotion or a thought because "s" and "f" are so nearly alike?

Is it not enough that I, an impulsive American, accustomed to do a thing first, and reflect upon it afterwards, must grope my way through a blind alley of substantives and adjectives, only to find the verb of action in an obscure corner, without ruining my eyesight in the groping?

But I dismiss these abstract reflections for a fresh and active resentment. This is the fifth or sixth dog that has passed my Spion, harnessed to a small barrow-like cart, and tugging painfully at a burden so ludicrously disproportionate to his size, that it would seem a burlesque, but for the poor dog's sad sincerity. Perhaps it is because I have the barbarian's fondness for dogs, and for their lawless, gentle, loving uselessness, that I rebel against this unnatural servitude. It seems as monstrous as if a child were put between the shafts, and made to carry burdens; and I have come to regard those men and women, who in the weakest perfunctory way affect to aid the poor brute by laying idle hands on the barrow behind, as I would unnatural parents. Pegasus harnessed to the Thracian herdsman's plough was no more of a desecration. I fancy the poor dog seems to feel the monstrosity of the performance, and, in sheer shame for his master, forgivingly tries to assume it is PLAY; and I have seen a little "colley" running along, barking, and endeavoring to leap and gambol in the shafts, before a load that any one out of this locality would have thought the direst cruelty. Nor do the older or more powerful dogs seem to become accustomed to it. When his cruel taskmaster halts with his wares, instantly the dog, either by sitting down in his harness, or crawling over the shafts, or by some unmistakable dog-like trick, utterly scatters any such delusion of even the habit of servitude. The few of his race who do not work in this ducal city seem to have lost their democratic canine sympathies, and look upon him with something of that indifferent calm with which yonder officer eyes the road-mender in the ditch below him. He loses even the characteristics of species. The common cur and mastiff look alike in harness. The burden levels all distinctions. I have said that he was generally sincere in his efforts. I recall but one instance to the contrary. I remember a young colley who first attracted my attention by his persistent barking. Whether he did this, as the plough-boy whistled, "for want of thought," or whether it was a running protest against his occupation, I could not determine, until one day I noticed, that, in barking, he slightly threw up his neck and shoulders, and that the two-wheeled barrow-like vehicle behind him, having its weight evenly poised on the wheels by the trucks in the hands of its driver, enabled him by this movement to cunningly throw the center of gravity and the greater weight on the man,--a fact which that less sagacious brute never discerned. Perhaps I am using a strong expression regarding his driver. It may be that the purely animal wants of the dog, in the way of food, care, and shelter, are more bountifully supplied in servitude than in freedom; becoming a valuable and useful property, he may be cared for and protected as such (an odd recollection that this argument had been used forcibly in regard to human slavery in my own country strikes me here); but his picturesqueness and poetry are gone, and I cannot help thinking that the people who have lost this gentle, sympathetic, characteristic figure from their domestic life and surroundings have not acquired an equal gain through his harsh labors.

To the American eye there is, throughout the length and breadth of this foreign city, no more notable and striking object than the average German houseservant. It is not that she has passed my Spion a dozen times within the last hour,--for here she is messenger, porter, and commissionnaire, as well as housemaid and cook,--but that she is always a phenomenon to the American stranger, accustomed to be abused in his own country by his foreign Irish handmaiden. Her presence is as refreshing and grateful as the morning light, and as inevitable and regular. When I add that with the novelty of being well served is combined the satisfaction of knowing that you have in your household an intelligent being who reads and writes with fluency, and yet does not abstract your books, nor criticise your literary composition; who is cleanly clad, and neat in her person, without the suspicion of having borrowed her mistress's dresses; who may be good-looking without the least imputation of coquetry or addition to her followers; who is obedient without servility, polite without flattery, willing and replete with supererogatory performance, without the expectation of immediate pecuniary return, what wonder that the American householder translated into German life feels himself in a new Eden of domestic possibilities unrealized in any other country, and begins to believe in a present and future of domestic happiness! What wonder that the American bachelor living in German lodgings feels half the terrors of the conjugal future removed, and rushes madly into love--and housekeeping! What wonder that I, a long-suffering and patient master, who have been served by the reticent but too imitative Chinaman; who have been "Massa" to the childlike but untruthful negro; who have been the recipient of the brotherly but uncertain ministrations of the South-Sea Islander, and have been proudly disregarded by the American aborigine, only in due time to meet the fate of my countrymen at the hands of Bridget the Celt,--what wonder that I gladly seize this opportunity to sing the praises of my German handmaid! Honor to thee, Lenchen, wherever thou goest! Heaven bless thee in thy walks abroad! whether with that tightly-booted cavalryman in thy Sunday gown and best, or in blue polka-dotted apron and bare head as thou trottest nimbly on mine errands,-- errands which Bridget o'Flaherty would scorn to undertake, or, undertaking, would hopelessly blunder in. Heaven bless thee, child, in thy early risings and in thy later sittings, at thy festive board overflowing with Essig and Fett, in the mysteries of thy Kuchen, in the fulness of thy Bier, and in thy nightly suffocations beneath mountainous and multitudinous feathers! Good, honest, simple-minded, cheerful, duty-loving Lenchen! Have not thy brothers, strong and dutiful as thou, lent their gravity and earnestness to sweeten and strengthen the fierce youth of the Republic beyond the seas? and shall not thy children inherit the broad prairies that still wait for them, and discover the fatness thereof, and send a portion transmuted in glittering shekels back to thee?

Almost as notable are the children whose round faces have as frequently been reflected in my Spion. Whether it is only a fancy of mine that the average German retains longer than any other race his childish simplicity and unconsciousness, or whether it is because I am more accustomed to the extreme self-assertion and early maturity of American children, I know not; but I am inclined to believe that among no other people is childhood as perennial, and to be studied in such characteristic and quaint and simple phases as here. The picturesqueness of Spanish and Italian childhood has a faint suspicion of the pantomime and the conscious attitudinizing of the Latin races. German children are not exuberant or volatile: they are serious,- -a seriousness, however, not to be confounded with the grave reflectiveness of age, but only the abstract wonderment of childhood; for all those who have made a loving study of the young human animal will, I think, admit that its dominant expression is GRAVITY, and not playfulness, and will be satisfied that he erred pitifully who first ascribed "light-heartedness" and "thoughtlessness" as part of its phenomena. These little creatures I meet upon the street,--whether in quaint wooden shoes and short woollen petticoats, or neatly booted and furred, with school knapsacks jauntily borne upon little square shoulders,--all carry likewise in their round chubby faces their profound wonderment and astonishment at the big busy world into which they have so lately strayed. If I stop to speak with this little maid who scarcely reaches to the top-boots of yonder cavalry officer, there is less of bashful self-consciousness in her sweet little face than of grave wonder at the foreign accent and strange ways of this new figure obtruded upon her limited horizon. She answers honestly, frankly, prettily, but gravely. There is a remote possibility that I might bite; and, with this suspicion plainly indicated in her round blue eyes, she quietly slips her little red hand from mine, and moves solemnly away. I remember once to have stopped in the street with a fair countrywoman of mine to interrogate a little figure in sabots,--the one quaint object in the long, formal perspective of narrow, gray bastard-Italian facaded houses of a Rhenish German Strasse. The sweet little figure wore a dark-blue woollen petticoat that came to its knees; gray woollen stockings covered the shapely little limbs below; and its very blonde hair, the color of a bright dandelion, was tied in a pathetic little knot at the back of its round head, and garnished with an absurd green ribbon. Now, although this gentlewoman's sympathies were catholic and universal, unfortunately their expression was limited to her own mother-tongue. She could not help pouring out upon the child the maternal love that was in her own womanly breast, nor could she withhold the "baby-talk" through which it was expressed. But, alas! it was in English. Hence ensued a colloquy, tender and extravagant on the part of the elder, grave and wondering on the part of the child. But the lady had a natural feminine desire for reciprocity, particularly in the presence of our emotion-scorning sex, and as a last resource she emptied the small silver of her purse into the lap of the coy maiden. It was a declaration of love, susceptible of translation at the nearest cake-shop. But the little maid, whose dress and manner certainly did not betray an habitual disregard of gifts of this kind, looked at the coin thoughtfully, but not regretfully. Some innate sense of duty, equally strong with that of being polite to strangers, filled her consciousness. With the utterly unexpected remark that her father 'did not allow her to take money', the queer little figure moved away, leaving the two Americans covered with mortification. The rare American child who could have done this would have done it with an attitude. This little German bourgeoise did it naturally. I do not intend to rush to the deduction that German children of the lower classes habitually refuse pecuniary gratuities: indeed, I remember to have wickedly suggested to my companion, that, to avoid impoverishment in a foreign land, she should not repeat the story nor the experiment. But I simply offer it as a fact, and to an American, at home or abroad, a novel one.

I owe to these little figures another experience quite as strange. It was at the close of a dull winter's day,--a day from which all out-of-door festivity seemed to be naturally excluded: there was a baleful promise of snow in the air and a dismal reminiscence of it under foot, when suddenly, in striking contrast with the dreadful bleakness of the street, a half dozen children, masked and bedizened with cheap ribbons, spangles, and embroidery, flashed across my Spion. I was quick to understand the phenomenon. It was the Carnival season. Only the night before I had been to the great opening masquerade,--a famous affair, for which this art-loving city is noted, and to which strangers are drawn from all parts of the Continent. I remember to have wondered if the pleasure-loving German in America had not broken some of his conventional shackles in emigration; for certainly I had found the Carnival balls of the "Lieder Kranz Society" in New York, although decorous and fashionable to the American taste, to be wild dissipations compared with the practical seriousness of this native performance, and I hailed the presence of these children in the open street as a promise of some extravagance, real, untrammelled, and characteristic. I seized my hat and--OVERCOAT,--a dreadful incongruity to the spangles that had whisked by, and followed the vanishing figures round the corner. Here they were re-enforced by a dozen men and women, fantastically, but not expensively arrayed, looking not unlike the supernumeraries of some provincial opera troupe. Following the crowd, which already began to pour in from the side-streets, in a few moments I was in the broad, grove-like allee, and in the midst of the masqueraders.

I remember to have been told that this was a characteristic annual celebration of the lower classes, anticipated with eagerness, and achieved with difficulty, indeed, often only through the alternative of pawning clothing and furniture to provide the means for this ephemeral transformation. I remember being warned, also, that the buffoonery was coarse, and some of the slang hardly fit for "ears polite." But I am afraid that I was not shocked at the prodigality of these poor people, who purchased a holiday on such hard conditions; and, as to the coarseness of the performance, I felt that I certainly might go where these children could.

At first the masquerading figures appeared to be mainly composed of young girls of ages varying from nine to eighteen. Their costumes--if what was often only the addition of a broad, bright-colored stripe to the hem of a short dress could be called a COSTUME--were plain, and seemed to indicate no particular historical epoch or character. A general suggestion of the peasant's holiday attire was dominant in all the costumes. Everybody was closely masked. All carried a short, gayly-striped baton of split wood, called a Pritsche, which, when struck sharply on the back or shoulders of some spectator or sister-masker, emitted a clattering, rasping sound. To wander hand in hand down this broad allee, to strike almost mechanically, and often monotonously, at each other with their batons, seemed to be the extent of that wild dissipation. The crowd thickened. Young men with false noses, hideous masks, cheap black or red cotton dominoes, soldiers in uniform, crowded past each other, up and down the promenade, all carrying a Pritsche, and exchanging blows with each other, but always with the same slow seriousness of demeanor, which, with their silence, gave the performance the effect of a religious rite. Occasionally some one shouted: perhaps a dozen young fellows broke out in song; but the shout was provocative of nothing, the song faltered as if the singers were frightened at their own voices. One blithe fellow, with a bear's head on his fur-capped shoulders, began to dance; but, on the crowd stopping to observe him seriously, he apparently thought better of it, and slipped away. Nevertheless, the solemn beating of Pritschen over each other's backs went on. I remember that I was followed the whole length of the allee by a little girl scarcely twelve years old, in a bright striped skirt and black mask, who from time to time struck me over the shoulders with a regularity and sad persistency that was peculiarly irresistible to me; the more so, as I could not help thinking that it was not half as amusing to herself. Once only did the ordinary brusque gallantry of the Carnival spirit show itself. A man with an enormous pair of horns, like a half-civilized satyr, suddenly seized a young girl and endeavored to kiss her. A slight struggle ensued, in which I fancied I detected in the girl's face and manner the confusion and embarrassment of one who was obliged to overlook, or seem to accept, a familiarity that was distasteful, rather than be laughed at for prudishness or ignorance. But the incident was exceptional. Indeed, it was particularly notable to my American eyes to find such decorum where there might easily have been the greatest license. I am afraid that an American mob of this class would have scarcely been as orderly and civil under the circumstances. They might have shown more humor; but there would have probably been more effrontery: they might have been more exuberant; they would certainly have been drunker. I did not notice a single masquerader unduly excited by liquor: there was not a word or motion from the lighter sex that could have been construed into an impropriety. There was something almost pathetic to me in this attempt to wrest gayety and excitement out of these dull materials; to fight against the blackness of that wintry sky, and the stubborn hardness of the frozen soil, with these painted sticks of wood; to mock the dreariness of their poverty with these flaunting raiments. It did not seem like them, or rather, consistent with my idea of them. There was incongruity deeper than their bizarre externals; a half-melancholy, half-crazy absurdity in their action, the substitution of a grim spasmodic frenzy for levity, that rightly or wrongly impressed me. When the increasing gloom of the evening made their figures undistinguishable, I turned into the first cross-street. As I lifted my hat to my persistent young friend with the Pritsche, I fancied she looked as relieved as myself. If, however, I was mistaken; if that child's pathway through life be strewn with rosy recollections of the unresisting back of the stranger American; if any burden, O Gretchen! laid upon thy young shoulders, be lighter for the trifling one thou didst lay upon mine,--know, then, that I, too, am content.

And so, day by day, has my Spion reflected the various changing forms of life before it. It has seen the first flush of spring in the broad allee, when the shadows of tiny leaflets overhead were beginning to checker the cool, square flagstones. It has seen the glare and fulness of summer sunshine and shadow, the flying of November gold through the air, the gaunt limbs, and stark, rigid, death-like whiteness of winter. It has seen children in their queer, wicker baby-carriages, old men and women, and occasionally that grim usher of death, in sable cloak and cocked hat,--a baleful figure for the wandering invalid tourist to meet,--who acts as undertaker for this ducal city, and marshals the last melancholy procession. I well remember my first meeting with this ominous functionary. It was an early autumnal morning; so early, that the long formal perspective of the allee, and the decorous, smooth vanishing-lines of cream-and-gray fronted houses, were unrelieved by a single human figure. Suddenly a tall black spectre, as theatrical and as unreal as the painted scenic distance, turned the corner from a cross-street, and moved slowly towards me. A long black cloak, falling from its shoulders to its feet, floated out on either side like sable wings; a cocked hat trimmed with crape, and surmounted by a hearse-like feather, covered a passionless face; and its eyes, looking neither left nor right, were fixed fatefully upon some distant goal. Stranger as I was to this Continental ceremonial figure, there was no mistaking his functions as the grim messenger, knocking "with equal foot" on every door; and, indeed, so perfectly did he act and look his role, that there was nothing ludicrous in the extraordinary spectacle. Facial expression and dignity of bearing were perfect; the whole man seemed saturated with the accepted sentiment of his office. Recalling the half-confused and half-conscious ostentatious hypocrisy of the American sexton, the shameless absurdities of the English mutes and mourners, I could not help feeling, that, if it were demanded that Grief and Fate should be personified, it were better that it should be well done. And it is one observation of my Spion, that this sincerity and belief is the characteristic of all Continental functionaries.

It is possible that my Spion has shown me little that is really characteristic of the people, and the few observations I have made I offer only as an illustration of the impressions made upon two-thirds of American strangers in the larger towns of Germany. Assimilation goes on more rapidly than we are led to imagine. As I have seen my friend Karl, fresh and awkward in his first uniform, lounging later down the allee with the blase listlessness of a full-blown militaire, so I have seen American and English residents gradually lose their peculiarities, and melt and merge into the general mass. Returning to my Spion after a flying trip through Belgium and France, as I look down the long perspective of the Strasse, I am conscious of recalling the same style of architecture and humanity at Aachen, Brussels, Lille, and Paris, and am inclined to believe that, even as I would have met, in a journey of the same distance through a parallel of the same latitude in America, a greater diversity of type and character, and a more distinct flavor of locality, even so would I have met a more heterogeneous and picturesque display from a club window on Fifth Avenue, New York, or Montgomery Street, San Francisco.

The Codes Of Hammurabi And Moses
W. W. Davies

QTY

The discovery of the Hammurabi Code is one of the greatest achievements of archaeology, and is of paramount interest, not only to the student of the Bible, but also to all those interested in ancient history...

Religion   **ISBN: *1-59462-338-4***   **Pages:132**
MSRP $12.95

The Theory of Moral Sentiments
Adam Smith

QTY

This work from 1749. contains original theories of conscience amd moral judgment and it is the foundation for systemof morals.

Philosophy **ISBN: *1-59462-777-0***   **Pages:536**
MSRP $19.95

Jessica's First Prayer
Hesba Stretton

QTY

In a screened and secluded corner of one of the many railway-bridges which span the streets of London there could be seen a few years ago, from five o'clock every morning until half past eight, a tidily set-out coffee-stall, consisting of a trestle and board, upon which stood two large tin cans, with a small fire of charcoal burning under each so as to keep the coffee boiling during the early hours of the morning when the work-people were thronging into the city on their way to their daily toil...

Childrens   **ISBN: *1-59462-373-2***   **Pages:84**
MSRP $9.95

My Life and Work
Henry Ford

QTY

Henry Ford revolutionized the world with his implementation of mass production for the Model T automobile. Gain valuable business insight into his life and work with his own auto-biography... "We have only started on our development of our country we have not as yet, with all our talk of wonderful progress, done more than scratch the surface. The progress has been wonderful enough but..."

Biographies/   **ISBN: *1-59462-198-5***   **Pages:300**
MSRP $21.95

The Art of Cross-Examination
Francis Wellman

QTY

I presume it is the experience of every author, after his first book is published upon an important subject, to be almost overwhelmed with a wealth of ideas and illustrations which could readily have been included in his book, and which to his own mind, at least, seem to make a second edition inevitable. Such certainly was the case with me; and when the first edition had reached its sixth impression in five months, I rejoiced to learn that it seemed to my publishers that the book had met with a sufficiently favorable reception to justify a second and considerably enlarged edition. ..

Reference   **ISBN: *1-59462-647-2***   **Pages:412**   *MSRP $19.95*

On the Duty of Civil Disobedience
Henry David Thoreau

QTY

Thoreau wrote his famous essay, On the Duty of Civil Disobedience, as a protest against an unjust but popular war and the immoral but popular institution of slave-owning. He did more than write—he declined to pay his taxes, and was hauled off to gaol in consequence. Who can say how much this refusal of his hastened the end of the war and of slavery ?

Law   **ISBN: *1-59462-747-9***   **Pages:48**   *MSRP $7.45*

Dream Psychology Psychoanalysis for Beginners
Sigmund Freud

QTY

Sigmund Freud, born Sigismund Schlomo Freud (May 6, 1856 - September 23, 1939), was a Jewish-Austrian neurologist and psychiatrist who co-founded the psychoanalytic school of psychology. Freud is best known for his theories of the unconscious mind, especially involving the mechanism of repression; his redefinition of sexual desire as mobile and directed towards a wide variety of objects; and his therapeutic techniques, especially his understanding of transference in the therapeutic relationship and the presumed value of dreams as sources of insight into unconscious desires.

Dream Psychology
Psychoanalysis for Beginners

Sigmund Freud

Psychology   **ISBN: *1-59462-905-6***   **Pages:196**   *MSRP $15.45*

The Miracle of Right Thought
Orison Swett Marden

QTY

Believe with all of your heart that you will do what you were made to do. When the mind has once formed the habit of holding cheerful, happy, prosperous pictures, it will not be easy to form the opposite habit. It does not matter how improbable or how far away this realization may see, or how dark the prospects may be, if we visualize them as best we can, as vividly as possible, hold tenaciously to them and vigorously struggle to attain them, they will gradually become actualized, realized in the life. But a desire, a longing without endeavor, a yearning abandoned or held indifferently will vanish without realization.

Pages:360

Self Help   **ISBN: *1-59462-644-8***   *MSRP $25.45*

The Rosicrucian Cosmo-Conception Mystic Christianity *by Max Heindel* ISBN: *1-59462-188-8* **$38.95**
The Rosicrucian Cosmo-conception is not dogmatic, neither does it appeal to any other authority than the reason of the student. It is: not controversial, but is: sent forth in the, hope that it may help to clear... New Age/Religion Pages 646

Abandonment To Divine Providence *by Jean-Pierre de Caussade* ISBN: *1-59462-228-0* **$25.95**
"The Rev. Jean Pierre de Caussade was one of the most remarkable spiritual writers of the Society of Jesus in France in the 18th Century. His death took place at Toulouse in 1751. His works have gone through many editions and have been republished... Inspirational/Religion Pages 400

Mental Chemistry *by Charles Haanel* ISBN: *1-59462-192-6* **$23.95**
Mental Chemistry allows the change of material conditions by combining and appropriately utilizing the power of the mind. Much like applied chemistry creates something new and unique out of careful combinations of chemicals the mastery of mental chemistry... New Age Pages 354

The Letters of Robert Browning and Elizabeth Barret Barrett 1845-1846 vol II ISBN: *1-59462-193-4* **$35.95**
by Robert Browning and Elizabeth Barrett Biographies Pages 596

Gleanings In Genesis (volume I) *by Arthur W. Pink* ISBN: *1-59462-130-6* **$27.45**
Appropriately has Genesis been termed "the seed plot of the Bible" for in it we have, in germ form, almost all of the great doctrines which are afterwards fully developed in the books of Scripture which follow... Religion/Inspirational Pages 420

The Master Key *by L. W. de Laurence* ISBN: *1-59462-001-6* **$30.95**
In no branch of human knowledge has there been a more lively increase of the spirit of research during the past few years than in the study of Psychology, Concentration and Mental Discipline. The requests for authentic lessons in Thought Control, Mental Discipline and... New Age/Business Pages 422

The Lesser Key Of Solomon Goetia *by L. W. de Laurence* ISBN: *1-59462-092-X* **$9.95**
This translation of the first book of the "Lernegton" which is now for the first time made accessible to students of Talismanic Magic was done, after careful collation and edition, from numerous Ancient Manuscripts in Hebrew, Latin, and French... New Age/Occult Pages 92

Rubaiyat Of Omar Khayyam *by Edward Fitzgerald* ISBN:*1-59462-332-5* **$13.95**
Edward Fitzgerald, whom the world has already learned, in spite of his own efforts to remain within the shadow of anonymity, to look upon as one of the rarest poets of the century, was born at Bredfield, in Suffolk, on the 31st of March, 1809. He was the third son of John Purcell... Music Pages 172

Ancient Law *by Henry Maine* ISBN: *1-59462-128-4* **$29.95**
The chief object of the following pages is to indicate some of the earliest ideas of mankind, as they are reflected in Ancient Law, and to point out the relation of those ideas to modern thought. Religiom/History Pages 452

Far-Away Stories *by William J. Locke* ISBN: *1-59462-129-2* **$19.45**
"Good wine needs no bush, but a collection of mixed vintages does. And this book is just such a collection. Some of the stories I do not want to remain buried for ever in the museum files of dead magazine-numbers an author's not unpardonable vanity..." Fiction Pages 272

Life of David Crockett *by David Crockett* ISBN: *1-59462-250-7* **$27.45**
"Colonel David Crockett was one of the most remarkable men of the times in which he lived. Born in humble life, but gifted with a strong will, an indomitable courage, and unremitting perseverance... Biographies/New Age Pages 424

Lip-Reading *by Edward Nitchie* ISBN: *1-59462-206-X* **$25.95**
Edward B. Nitchie, founder of the New York School for the Hard of Hearing, now the Nitchie School of Lip-Reading, Inc, wrote "LIP-READING Principles and Practice". The development and perfecting of this meritorious work on lip-reading was an undertaking... How-to Pages 400

A Handbook of Suggestive Therapeutics, Applied Hypnotism, Psychic Science ISBN: *1-59462-214-0* **$24.95**
by Henry Munro Health/New Age/Health/Self-help Pages 376

A Doll's House: and Two Other Plays *by Henrik Ibsen* ISBN: *1-59462-112-8* **$19.95**
Henrik Ibsen created this classic when in revolutionary 1848 Rome. Introducing some striking concepts in playwriting for the realist genre, this play has been studied the world over. Fiction/Classics/Plays 308

The Light of Asia *by sir Edwin Arnold* ISBN: *1-59462-204-3* **$13.95**
In this poetic masterpiece, Edwin Arnold describes the life and teachings of Buddha. The man who was to become known as Buddha to the world was born as Prince Gautama of India but he rejected the worldly riches and abandoned the reigns of power when... Religion/History/Biographies Pages 170

The Complete Works of Guy de Maupassant *by Guy de Maupassant* ISBN: *1-59462-157-8* **$16.95**
"For days and days, nights and nights, I had dreamed of that first kiss which was to consecrate our engagement, and I knew not on what spot I should put my lips..." Fiction/Classics Pages 240

The Art of Cross-Examination *by Francis L. Wellman* ISBN: *1-59462-309-0* **$26.95**
Written by a renowned trial lawyer, Wellman imparts his experience and uses case studies to explain how to use psychology to extract desired information through questioning. How-to/Science/Reference Pages 408

Answered or Unanswered? *by Louisa Vaughan* ISBN: *1-59462-248-5* **$10.95**
Miracles of Faith in China Religion Pages 112

The Edinburgh Lectures on Mental Science (1909) *by Thomas* ISBN: *1-59462-008-3* **$11.95**
This book contains the substance of a course of lectures recently given by the writer in the Queen Street Hall, Edinburgh. Its purpose is to indicate the Natural Principles governing the relation between Mental Action and Material Conditions... New Age/Psychology Pages 148

Ayesha *by H. Rider Haggard* ISBN: *1-59462-301-5* **$24.95**
Verily and indeed it is the unexpected that happens! Probably if there was one person upon the earth from whom the Editor of this, and of a certain previous history, did not expect to hear again... Classics Pages 380

Ayala's Angel *by Anthony Trollope* ISBN: *1-59462-352-X* **$29.95**
The two girls were both pretty, but Lucy who was twenty-one who supposed to be simple and comparatively unattractive, whereas Ayala was credited, as her Bombwhat romantic name might show, with poetic charm and a taste for romance. Ayala when her father died was nineteen... Fiction Pages 484

The American Commonwealth *by James Bryce* ISBN: *1-59462-286-8* **$34.45**
An interpretation of American democratic political theory. It examines political mechanics and society from the perspective of Scotsman James Bryce Politics Pages 572

Stories of the Pilgrims *by Margaret P. Pumphrey* ISBN: *1-59462-116-0* **$17.95**
This book explores pilgrims religious oppression in England as well as their escape to Holland and eventual crossing to America on the Mayflower, and their early days in New England... History Pages 268

QTY

The Fasting Cure *by Sinclair Upton*   ISBN: *1-59462-222-1*   **$13.95**

In the Cosmopolitan Magazine for May, 1910, and in the Contemporary Review (London) for April, 1910, I published an article dealing with my experiences in fasting. I have written a great many magazine articles, but never one which attracted so much attention... New Age/Self Help/Health Pages 164

Hebrew Astrology *by Sepharial*   ISBN: *1-59462-308-2*   **$13.45**

In these days of advanced thinking it is a matter of common observation that we have left many of the old landmarks behind and that we are now pressing forward to greater heights and to a wider horizon than that which represented the mind-content of our progenitors... Astrology Pages 144

Thought Vibration or The Law of Attraction in the Thought World   ISBN: *1-59462-127-6*   **$12.95**

by William Walker Atkinson   Psychology/Religion Pages 144

Optimism *by Helen Keller*   ISBN: *1-59462-108-X*   **$15.95**

Helen Keller was blind, deaf, and mute since 19 months old, yet famously learned how to overcome these handicaps, communicate with the world, and spread her lectures promoting optimism. An inspiring read for everyone... Biographies/Inspirational Pages 84

Sara Crewe *by Frances Burnett*   ISBN: *1-59462-360-0*   **$9.45**

In the first place, Miss Minchin lived in London. Her home was a large, dull, tall one, in a large, dull square, where all the houses were alike, and all the sparrows were alike, and where all the door-knockers made the same heavy sound... Childrens/Classic Pages 88

The Autobiography of Benjamin Franklin *by Benjamin Franklin*   ISBN: *1-59462-135-7*   **$24.95**

The Autobiography of Benjamin Franklin has probably been more extensively read than any other American historical work, and no other book of its kind has had such ups and downs of fortune. Franklin lived for many years in England, where he was agent... Biographies/History Pages 332

Name	
Email	
Telephone	
Address	
City, State ZIP	

☐ **Credit Card**   ☐ **Check / Money Order**

Credit Card Number	
Expiration Date	
Signature	

Please Mail to: Book Jungle
PO Box 2226
Champaign, IL 61825
or Fax to: 630-214-0564

ORDERING INFORMATION

web: *www.bookjungle.com*
email: *sales@bookjungle.com*
fax: *630-214-0564*
mail: *Book Jungle PO Box 2226 Champaign, IL 61825*
or PayPal *to sales@bookjungle.com*

Please contact us for bulk discounts

DIRECT-ORDER TERMS

**20% Discount if You Order
Two or More Books**
Free Domestic Shipping!
Accepted: Master Card, Visa,
Discover, American Express

www.ingramcontent.com/pod-product-compliance
Lightning Source LLC
Chambersburg PA
CBHW080835250626
47160CB00008B/2938